# The Subway Stops at BRYANT PARK

# The Subway Stops at BRYANT PARK

## N. West Moss

**Stories**

*Leapfrog Press*
*Fredonia, New York*

Published in 2017 in the United States by
Leapfrog Press LLC
PO Box 505
Fredonia, NY 14063
www.leapfrogpress.com

Printed in the United States of America

Distributed in the United States by
Consortium Book Sales and Distribution
St. Paul, Minnesota 55114
www.cbsd.com

Author photo courtesy of Mahmoud Sami
Illustrations from photographs by N. West Moss
New York City Transit Authority token illustration by Laura Oakes

First Edition

Library of Congress Cataloging-in-Publication Data

Names: Moss, N. West, author.
Title: The subway stops at Bryant Park / N. West Moss.
Description: First edition. | Fredonia, NY : Leapfrog Press, 2017.
Identifiers: LCCN 2017010653 (print) | LCCN 2016054399 (ebook) | ISBN
9781935248910 (paperback) | ISBN 9781935248927 (epub)
Subjects: LCSH: City dwellers--Fiction. | City and town life--Fiction. |
Urban parks--Fiction. | Bryant Park (New York, N.Y.)--Fiction. | New York
(N.Y.)--Fiction. | BISAC: FICTION / Short Stories (single author). |
FICTION / Literary. | FICTION / Urban Life. | FICTION / Cultural Heritage.
Classification: LCC PS3613.O77967 A6 2017 (ebook) | LCC PS3613.O77967
(print)
| DDC 813/.6--dc23
LC record available at https://lccn.loc.gov/2017010653

To my mother –
a fine artist and close friend
who has flung her arms wide to my writing for a lifetime;

and

To my father –
who bought me a typewriter for my 9th birthday,
and then begged me to stop typing so everyone could sleep.

# Introduction

Just as Fitzgerald focused his writing on the Northeast (which he adopted in prep school), and Salinger focused on his native New York City, N. West Moss has further zoomed in on Bryant Park in midtown Manhattan. More than simply a setting, the park serves as a vivid character in her contemplative short story collection, *The Subway Stops at Bryant Park*.

As the Bryant Park Corporation fixed the numerous problems visiting the park over the years—violence, poor maintenance, the crumbling bones of its infrastructure—my father aimed to make the park into Manhattan's town square, central to the lives of those who lived, worked, and commuted through and around it. He's proud of books like this one by West, whose fascinating short stories capture the importance of the park in the lives of its neighbors.

West and her father Lloyd Moss, an important part of New York City's cultural life for decades in his role as a classical music host for WQXR, spent many hours together in Bryant Park over the years. West's collection is especially vibrant to us, as a father and daughter to whom the park has played a similar role.

Bryant Park has left an indelible mark on my father and me, just as it has on West's writing, trickling into her graceful phrases. Reading these stories, one can almost envision the soft greenery and pastel flower beds against the sharp backdrop of the buildings of midtown Manhattan.

We hope you will bring your copy to Bryant Park, drag a chair underneath the shade of the London plane trees, and lose yourself in the stories. West's words recognize the soil and take root, and you can watch her stories blossom in front of you.

Dan Biederman
Exec. Director & Founder
Bryant Park Corporation

Brooke Biederman
Author

# Contents

# The Subway Stops at BRYANT PARK

# Omeer's Mangoes

In the decades that Omeer had lived and worked across from Bryant Park, everything had changed for them both, for the park and for him. Omeer had married and had a son, and the marriage had devolved from love to disappointment to peace, finally settling into something that could be described most charitably as a kind of permanent calm. And the park. Well.

It had always been called Bryant Park, but when Omeer first arrived in New York City, the park was dangerous, avoided. His first New York friend, Angelo, who had been hired to polish the brass in the lobby of Omeer's building, told him that some people called it Needle Park. Angelo was wise, and waved his filter-less cigarette knowingly at homeless people sleeping in the park. "He lives there." He pointed with the burning end of his cigarette. "He washes in the fountain and uses the bushes as a toilet. You can smell it from here. And some of them push needles in their arms and when they nod off, the needles fall on the ground. It's a park that grows needles, see?" He laughed, two plumes of smoke pouring from his nostrils like a dragon.

Omeer, a doorman in a building that looked out on the park, watched from across the street as the prostitutes in stretchy, sparkling dresses came at night and walked on high heels up behind the hedges. It was a dark place in those years, a wasteland.

But none of it upset Omeer, who as a young man was full of hope, all forward momentum and open arms. New York City, even the park with the dirty condoms and sad women, thrilled him. He had a job and a uniform too, brown with brass buttons, and his tenants did not sleep in the park. His tenants back then were celebrities and artists, nice people who brought him coffee in the morning and seemed embarrassed to have the door held open for them day after day. The building, his building, was beautiful, so elegant with its wide marble staircase and brass elevator doors, polished every month by Angelo and his father. It did not matter that Needle Park was across the street. Omeer's building was an oasis of kindness and beauty that shamed the park, not the other way around.

The people in the building in those early decades were like Omeer's family. He knew which one was expecting a grandchild, which one was contemplating divorce. One tenant was a radio personality, another was an artist who always had paint in his hair, and one wrote music for the movies. Imagine that! They thanked him constantly and gave him tips at Christmas.

Omeer used to stand on the top step of the stoop at dawn and watch the park for rats beneath the boxwoods. He knew they were boxwoods because he had asked Mrs. Dennis from the 12th floor. She had been so beautiful then, too, a model for Clairol; her blond hair and face had been so sweet and pretty that Omeer turned away when she said hello. The Dennises were older than Omeer, and he thought of them with respect, as the stars who would play his parents in the movie version of his life, which would be set in New York City, not Iran, where he had been born.

Omeer's real father had once been a businessman, before they all left Iran and scattered. At first Omeer told him the truth about his work, about the building, the uniform, the clusters of grapes carved above the doorways in the lobby. His father seemed proud, thought it was a good beginning for his son. Omeer imagined his father telling his friends in England, where he had settled, that his son lived in New York City, that his son was a doorman who wore a uniform with polished brass buttons. His father offered Omeer advice on the phone the first Thursday of every month, about saving money and meeting Iranian girls in New York.

After Omeer's mother died, and it became clear that his father would never come to America, not even to visit, Omeer began to lie to him. His father wanted more for him than a doorman job, which had been fine for a few years, but was no longer enough. When Omeer told him he was looking for a new job, his father said, "Good man! You must always strive to better yourself," and Omeer remembered then how nice it was to be far away from his father's knack for success.

Omeer made up stories that his father could share with friends over cards, but Omeer's honest heart made him an unimaginative and nervous liar. He fabricated interviews he was going on, and outfits the interviewers wore, and because he wanted his father to think kindly of America, Omeer said that some of the interviewers expressed interest in Iran, and one even asked about Omeer's father, supposedly, which of course no one would ever have done.

This false interview period stretched to months, and in an attempt to keep the stories interesting, Omeer moved the interviews to restaurants, although Omeer had never eaten in a restaurant, other than the pizza place on the corner. He described one interview for his father, saying, "I ordered a steak and it came with three different kinds of potatoes and a bowl of apricots for dessert." He hesitated. "And pots of tea. Pots of hot, sweet tea." This was how Omeer thought someone in England by way of Iran might picture an American meal, different in the potatoes, but similar in the apricots and pots of tea.

He saved his money, ironing his own shirts, making cheese sandwiches in his tiny kitchen and eating them standing up with the TV on. He wanted a family, he told his father, and himself. Yes, he would love to have enough money one day to have a wife.

Finally, Omeer felt he had to tell his father that he had gotten a new job from all of these interviews he had gone on. He couldn't pretend to go on interviews forever, so he said that he had been hired at a bank, even though Omeer knew nothing about finance or banks or what kind of job he'd even get in one. Angelo said, "Tell him it's in public relations. Everyone works in public relations. Call it PR," which Omeer's father seemed to understand, even if Omeer did not. That was early still, in his first decade in New York, when Omeer made it a habit to sweep the sidewalk in front of the building very early, before his tenants even woke up, without even being asked.

It was after Omeer became a make-believe public relations agent at a bank that the park across the street began to change in earnest. It got roped off with police tape, and in rumbled cranes and dump trucks, dumpsters and jackhammers. Omeer and Angelo kept track of the tearing down and the carting away and then watched as the park was rebuilt. For four entire years the park was a noisy mess. Omeer and the other doormen swept and mopped every day to keep the dust from polluting their marble lobby.

Omeer read about the renovations in the paper. They were planning on lowering the park to ground level. Astonishing. Impossible. The papers said it was dangerous to have a park up higher than the street, because good people were too scared to go in. "If it's not at eye level," Angelo explained to him, "the police can't look in. It's like a secret world where all sorts of things can happen. You don't want to know." Angelo shook his head, took off his work hat and rubbed his hands through his hair to show how upsetting it was in there.

When Angelo's father retired, Angelo was put in charge of the family business, polishing the elevator doors, the brass bannisters that looped up the grand marble staircase, the handles on the front doors. He and Omeer stood outside so that Angelo could smoke, and later, after Angelo left, Omeer would sweep up the filter-less cigarette butts and matches he'd left on the ground.

Omeer read to Angelo from the newspaper about the park, while Angelo commented. "People hide in the park," said Angelo.

"Right," said Omeer, "the addicts and the hookers." He tried to sound disdainful, but it didn't work and he was embarrassed that he had said the word hooker out loud. Angelo had disdain for specific things: for sloppy carpentry, and for people who ate pizza while they walked down the street, but Omeer couldn't muster genuine disdain. It simply was not in his nature, although he tried.

When the construction was finally done and the dust was hosed off of the block, when the park had been successfully lowered, Omeer called it a work of art. "It's magnificent," he would murmur to his tenants as he held the front door for them and swept his hand across the vista, the marble handrails, the full flowerbeds. He realized he was bragging as though the park were his, and he blushed over and over again, but he couldn't stop paying compliments to it.

Men in green jumpsuits came next and put in more plants, thousands of them along with full-grown London plane trees. Stonemasons came too and fixed the paths and stone walls. Old statues were polished and new statues went in. Now, years later, gardeners were in the park every day in the spring and summer, and even into the fall, planting begonias and digging up daffodils that had just finished blooming, slipping hoses into each pot of flowers until the water ran over the top and soaked the slate beneath. There was a man in a green uniform whom Omeer knew by sight. He walked all day long pushing a garbage can on wheels. If someone let a napkin fall to the ground, the man was there, seconds later, to put it in his pail. If a leaf fell from a tree, he caught it.

The park became a testament to progress, to how things got steadily better over time, about humanity, like the opposite of entropy, where he had read that things naturally fall apart. It made Omeer tremendously hopeful, about the park, about his life. What they had done to the park was a triumph over entropy. He said that to Angelo, who shrugged.

Omeer got married the year the restaurant went into the park. What a shock it had been to his tenants to learn that there would be a place to have lunch and dinner right there, steps from their front door, butting up against the back of the New York Public

Library. Mrs. Dennis from the 12th floor said, "It's like living at Versailles," which Omeer had heard of. It made everyone in the building stand up a little straighter to have a park so lovely.

On Thursday nights the restaurant hosted a singles' night where skinny men and women in their tight business clothes came in waves. Omeer could see them through the glass of the front door, laughing with their mouths wide open, leaning in to one another, talking into their phones when their dates went to the rest room. Always busy, always important.

He walked over and studied the menu that hung in the window, and saw a bottle of wine for sale for $47. He felt rich just seeing that, proud that they thought so highly of themselves. The neighborhood had become as special as Omeer's beautiful marble-and-brass building, as if the building had finally succeeded in making the park behave.

He cut out newspaper articles about the park and sent them to his father, telling him that he went to the restaurant there for business lunches, that the bank let him put it on his expense account. He wished he hadn't lied to his father about being a banker, because he wanted to tell him how he had just been promoted to superintendent of the building, a big step up. His father would probably have been proud, would have congratulated him. When he got the promotion, Omeer had his doorman uniform cleaned professionally. He hung it in its dry-cleaning bag in the back of his closet in case he ever needed it again.

Omeer's wife was American, with enough Persian blood in her family history for him to consider her essentially Iranian. She was younger than he was, and shy when they first met. She moved into his apartment with him, the little one bedroom he had bought on the top floor when prices had been dirt-cheap. She bought paint the color of bricks and pomegranates and painted the walls. She put out a vase of fake flowers that looked real. To Omeer, she had the eye of an artist. He encouraged her in all of her early tentativeness. He took her to the park on his day off and showed her the menu hanging in the restaurant window, pointed at the $47 bottle of wine listed there, and they turned to each other and made shocked faces.

One day, a carousel appeared in the park, and reporters wrote stories about it, which Omeer cut out. But by then, his father had died and Omeer put the clippings from the newspapers in the bottom of his sock drawer with a heavy heart. It was the same year that his wife, grown less shy by this time, gave birth to their son. Progress, as it always had for Omeer, outweighed the setbacks. He had a son now. He had a family of his own.

And then, soon after that, at no particular moment, without being definite or clear, at a time seen only in retrospect as a moment, a year later or maybe two or three after the birth of his son, the pendulum of Omeer's life which had been swinging steadily forward along with the good fortune of Bryant Park, halted, stuttered, and began, ever so slowly, to swing backwards, as every life does eventually. As his up-hill resolved itself eventually into a downslope, the pendulum of the park continued its seemingly unstoppable upward trajectory.

As he grew older, Omeer had begun to worry about his graying hair. He became afraid of closed spaces, and in his late 40s began to sleep with the blinds open to let in the street light, fearful of the coffin-feeling of waking up swallowed by darkness. It annoyed his wife, who liked to sleep without interruptions from light or noise or, by then, from a hand reaching out for her in the night.

Omeer, unlike his wife, found sweetness in interruptions. Everything else was just a list of chores that repeated with the days of the week. Interruptions were the music. Omeer wanted to please his wife, and this made him worry about eating too much salt and drinking too much caffeine. He worried about his blood pressure because she told him to. "We're getting old," she said, filing down the nail on her index finger, although she did not look old. He had seen her gray hairs one morning over breakfast, but by that night, her hair was black again. "It's time you began to take care of yourself, Omeer." He liked it when she said his name.

Omeer was aware of his age. His tooth ached. His knee ached, but still he was surprised, over and over again, by his reflection in the glass front door of the building. He expected to see his shiny black hair, his eyes smiling back at him, but was forced instead to ask, "Who is that old man?" followed by, "Ah, this is who I've become."

All of New York City had changed too as Omeer grew older. Midtown had been "cleaned up," but the park, its transformation had been unimaginable, breathtaking, and Omeer had quietly borne witness as they began to offer free yoga classes in the park and French lessons. They held poetry readings and chess tournaments there. In summer they showed movies and offered free juggling classes. Juggling classes!

One winter it was announced that the park would house a skating rink. His wife didn't believe him at first. "They can't fit a skating rink in that little park," she said. So he brought her there, with their boy who was still in her arms then. They were both stunned, but there it was. "Visionaries," Omeer said. He and his wife clutched their son, making a fragile little family unit. They watched the people wheeling around the rink, bundled in their new clothes from the Gap, spotlights shining down on them as if they were gods. Omeer and his wife looked at each other and laughed then. It was not just a dream, Omeer knew, because the next year the rink came back and brought with it a Christmas tree as tall as a skyscraper. It took a truck with a ladder on it to hang the star on the tree's top.

As the park and the neighborhood blossomed, however, the kindness of the people seemed pushed to the side, as though kindness was the price that had to be paid for progress. Omeer, then, looked back on those early years, before the park had been renovated, with some nostalgia. Some of his good tenants moved out and new, driven ones moved in. The new ones wore ties and never looked up, and became annoyed quickly. Some of the old tenants remained, and as they aged, he cared for them like he would have cared for his own father, helping them into cabs, carrying their mail upstairs for them, bowing a tiny bit when they came in.

# Omeer's Mangoes

Mr. Dennis, for example, used to ride his bicycle all over Manhattan. He had been famous then on the radio, and Omeer told people, "He is an excellent man, a perfect man." But Mr. Dennis had grown old and slow like everyone else, and had finally collapsed in the lobby, nearly killing Omeer with shame and worry. He knelt next to him, murmuring, "Oh, Mr. Dennis, Mr. Dennis, I'm so sorry," too shy to take the man's hand. The people he admired disintegrated like everyone else, and it broke Omeer's heart. No one was immune.

Filling the park with flowers and trees and folding chairs, making it so beautiful, brought smart, angry tenants to Omeer's building—lawyers and traders from Wall Street. The new board president wore blue ties that were tied too tightly around his fat neck. His face was always red, strangled by his own ties, like a balloon about to pop. He looked at Omeer with suspicion, as though Omeer wasn't working hard enough, which caused Omeer to feel confused and apologetic. He took such pride in his work. Angelo told him only to sweep up when tenants were watching so they could see how hard he worked. It wasn't terrible advice.

A hotel went in next door to Omeer's building, and a magazine shop on the other side, next to a French coffee shop that sold pepper grinders and extra-virgin olive oil. The tenants got fancier too, wanted more things, had more packages delivered and cleaning women and guests arriving. People moved in and out more frequently.

Angelo still came, but they refused to raise his fee when they required him to polish the marble floor in addition to his other jobs, and so he was always in a rush too, like everyone else. The board president with the red face and tight neckties told Omeer that they were letting go of one of the other doormen, "to cut costs." Omeer would have to do his superintendent work during the day now, get his uniform out of the closet again to work occasional overnights, and "share the burden" as the board president told him, not making eye contact with Omeer. They didn't care that Omeer had a little boy. Times were hard. If he wanted to stay, to keep his apartment, this is what he'd have to do. Omeer considered it a demotion.

By the time Omeer's boy could make his own bowl of cereal in the morning without spilling the milk, Omeer's wife had lost her reticence entirely. Omeer became aware that his wife and son pitied him, and sometimes were angry at him for making them pity him, back and forth, pity, anger.

Omeer's hair had begun to come in gray by his temples, and his wife was bored at home, now that their boy didn't need much from her. She had friends too, American friends, and she told Omeer that she wanted to go back to school. So Omeer smiled, nodded, and mortgaged the apartment, the one that he had paid off completely, and he sent his wife to design school at Parsons. She took his hands in hers. "Thank you, Omeer." He loved it when she said his name. He had made her happy.

She studied hard and came home exhilarated. He was glad for her as if she were his growing daughter. When she graduated, he and their son went to the ceremony. At the coffee shop afterward, with her much younger school friends, one of them said, "The economy is not good for designers just starting out." His wife had shrugged.

She got a new hairstyle, even made her clothes for a bit on a sewing machine Omeer bought for her, but soon after she graduated and found the reality of getting a job to be quite different from the dream, she became disenchanted by the fashion shows that were still held in the park then.

"Oh!" she said, "The *beep beep beep* of those trucks backing up! How do they expect people to live here?"

After being demoted, Omeer went three years without a raise. Their bills went up, though, and they had a mortgage now. His wife was forced to take a part-time job at a dry cleaner's downtown, to her great dismay. He knew that her failure was his failure.

The board president with the blue ties and red face explained that they couldn't give raises, and not to expect one any time soon, either. "There are plenty of people who'd be happy to do your job for half of what you make," he told Omeer, which struck Omeer as probably true. He worked hard, though, and loyalty should count for something. Shouldn't it?

As his financial strains intensified, Omeer made sure to remain kind. It was not his wife's fault that she had married a man who would remain a doorman forever. When she came home with new lipstick, he told her how pretty she was. He did not want anything to make him like the board president with the tight ties. Being kind made him feel better. He loved how smart his wife was, how much she seemed to know. He liked her new long nails, and the way she tapped them gently against her coffee cup in the morning as she read the paper.

He felt guilty about his own graying hair, imagined that it embarrassed her and their boy. He asked her if she wanted him to dye it black and she laughed. "Why bother?" she said. He felt her recoil from her own comment, and she added, "You look distinguished like this." Omeer knew that she gave him the compliment because she didn't love him anymore. It wasn't her fault. Love just grew or failed, and her love for him had stalled out.

One day, his son came to him with a flyer from middle school that read "Summer Music Camp." He had been studying the saxophone, which caused Omeer distress. He didn't want the boy to practice when it would disturb tenants. But now this. He didn't have the $500 for music camp but wanted to say yes to the boy. He said, "Money's tight this year," and he saw the boy's eyes get small and suspicious.

"Mom gets to go out all the time," the boy said.

"Yes?" said Omeer.

"You are just a cheapskate," the boy said, and Omeer recognized the term as something his wife used.

Omeer was so ashamed that he went to the bank the next morning and took the $500 out of his almost-empty savings account. He told his son that he could go, that he had found the money. The boy shrugged, not believing him. "No," said Omeer, "I mean it. I am not a cheap steak." He knew immediately that he'd said it wrong. He made mistakes when he was nervous. He had pictured the conversation going so much better, had imagined that his boy would smile and thank him for his generosity, but now Omeer felt frantic and hopeless and embarrassed. The boy rolled his eyes and sighed derisively, and something came up out of Omeer's stomach and into his throat that he couldn't control. He didn't realize what he was doing until after he had slapped the boy *BAM!* across his cheek.

They stared at each other while the slap reverberated. Omeer knew it had happened because his hand stung, and because the boy's cheek bloomed pink. He wanted to apologize, wanted to beg the boy not to tell his mother, but instead Omeer took the elevator to the basement and stood in the dark near the incinerator, catching his breath, keeping the tears that gathered inside his eyes.

It was the summer of the slap that someone hired pianists to play music during lunch hour at Omeer's end of the park. The piano was on wheels so it could be moved around. Pianists came every weekday, a new one each week, and sat down at the piano with a flourish, playing show tunes and jazz and sometimes classical to entertain the crowds. Omeer took his lunch there almost every day. He listened right until the end, even if there was an encore, and then he'd rush across the street, up to his apartment, change into his doorman's uniform, and be at the front desk for the 3 o'clock shift.

Omeer recognized the park employees who cleaned the fountain who would sometimes stop and listen to the music too, leaning on their brooms. Their uniforms were green, like the color of the leaves, as though they grew there in the park, the workers.

He became aware of a woman who visited the park every Tuesday. She dragged a suitcase, wrapped entirely in Saran Wrap, and several purses, all wrapped in cellophane too. She wore a rain hat tied under her chin, and her lipstick went outside of the lines on her lips up to her nose almost. She would settle in by the piano and arrange her purses on separate chairs. Then she would unwrap a sandwich from a piece of tin foil and eat it.

24

# Omeer's Mangoes

She never made a sound, never caused a disturbance, always cleaned up after herself. She and Omeer were companions of sorts on Tuesdays that summer. As Omeer would be getting up to leave at the end of each Tuesday concert, she would be stacking her purses back on her suitcase and wheeling off toward home, her plastic kerchief tied tightly under her chin. She even pushed the chairs back in.

Omeer looked forward to that hour, rain or shine. It became his club, his piece of the park where he was better off than some, and not as well off as others. Even though he never spoke to people there, outside of a polite nod, he felt they were his friends, a kind of family that might have existed given better circumstances. How much they would like him if they knew him, he thought. How kind he'd be to them, laughing at their jokes. They wouldn't know that he was a disappointment, because he wouldn't tell them. He would not divulge how much money he owed, how he owed more on the apartment than it was worth, that his wife worked part time at a dry cleaner's. They would not know about him slapping his son, or hiding in the basement afterward. They would know the Omeer that he wished to be—kind, generous, loyal, appreciated.

He had a favorite table in the shade—close enough to hear the music but far enough away to watch the people, who came in colored scarves and high-heeled shoes and danced with their children under the pale green branches of the plane trees. They all spoke different languages, and like chips of glass in a kaleidoscope, whatever way they happened to fall, Omeer found beautiful—like his wife and son when they didn't know he was watching them.

When the long, hot month of August came, it brought a new woman to the piano concerts. She came barreling in one day, her shiny black hair pulled into a ponytail. Her clothes were runners' clothes, skintight and lime green. Her enormous fat rolls spilled out from underneath her shirt, smooth and round as a wet otter. Omeer was charmed. Her cheeks were round and glossy, and she shone, as though she had rubbed her skin with oil. She seemed quite alive. When Omeer pointed her out to Angelo one day, Angelo said, "She looks like a Samoan. I've read about them. They paddle canoes in the Arctic." Omeer looked up Samoan on his son's computer and was astonished at how wrong Angelo had been, but from then on Omeer thought of her as "the Samoan" anyway.

She came after that every so often, and Omeer was glad when she showed up, like a mountain had rolled in to keep the wind and sun off of his back. One day early on, she had a tight lemon-yellow shirt on that did not cover her belly, a strip of which was revealed, the color of polished teak. She put her belongings on one of the round tables and stood next to it, doing stretching exercises. Every time she reached up, her belly, hanging over her pants was exposed, rich and coffee-colored. She looked like a warrior to Omeer, or a fertility goddess.

She sat then and pulled a see-through plastic container full of sliced mangoes out of a bag. She burst with vitality, eating fruit for lunch, doing stretching exercises, her new sneakers a glowing talisman for physical fitness. It all seemed very Samoan to Omeer. She ate the mango with her fingers, licking them after each slice. She took a Wet-Nap out of her purse when she was done and carefully wiped her hands. Fastidious. Natural.

Each time she arrived, she stretched until her belly button was exposed. And when she stopped reaching, the shirt stayed up while she sat and ate her mangoes. Omeer was giddy over how unselfconscious she was, how brave and relaxed and accepting of her own self. He was so much the opposite that he used mouthwash every morning, every night, after every meal, and still his wife pulled away. But his Samoan, she left her fat belly exposed in the middle of the park, and he was sure that everyone who saw her must love her for her abandon.

One day she looked up from a dripping mango slice and caught Omeer's eye. She hesitated and then smiled wide to show all of her top teeth. He felt he had been caught staring at her, and he stood up, walking directly out of the park and up to his building, where he saw his reflection in the front door of his building. He was shocked, as though he had just seen himself for the first time in decades. How his eyelids drooped. How tight his pants were around his waist. He remembered a photograph of himself when he had been the Samoan's age, with a full head of shiny black hair. He had been handsome then, he now realized. His daydreams had allowed him to be mistaken about who he had become. Omeer had thought himself the man who might have known this girl once, been friends with her, if things had been different, if he had not married and accidentally grown old.

The next morning, Omeer went to the deli and bought himself a little container of sliced mangoes, and the cashier gave him a plastic fork. He hadn't eaten a mango since he was a little boy, and he ate them now for lunch by the piano, one at a time. The mango was strange, fibrous and sweet, and full of vague, echo-y memories from what felt like a life that once belonged to some-one else, someone who had lived a hundred years ago. It was not enough food for him, and he knew he'd be hungry that night be-hind the front desk, and he was disappointed that the Samoan woman wasn't there to see him.

The next day, at the same deli, Omeer bought himself a box of men's hair dye, the kind that promised to subtly cover only some of the gray, to make him look just a bit younger. He hid the box in the drawer by his bed and dyed his hair when his wife and son had gone out. Some of the dye splattered on the wall by the light switch. He scrubbed it with his toothbrush and got the spot off, but the toothbrush was ruined.

When Omeer took the towel off of his head, he wasn't certain, but he sensed he looked different, very subtly so. It made his eyes look more blue, he thought, turning his head from side to side in front of the mirror. It left some of the gray, maybe almost all of it, he couldn't tell, which he found tasteful. He had been worried that the change would be alarming, too severe, but it wasn't. How could anyone accuse him of dyeing his hair when there were patches of gray still in it?

He wrapped his toothbrush and the box from the hair dye in a plastic bag, and instead of throwing it down the garbage chute by the elevator, he carried it down and put it in a garbage can on the street. He went back to the deli to get mangoes for lunch again. Yes, he had been hungry the night before, but perhaps it was not the end of the world to be a bit hungry. He could stand to lose a few pounds, and mangoes were delicious, he had decided. They tasted the way perfume smelled.

To his delight, the Samoan girl was already there when Omeer took his seat. The pianist was playing something that sounded like a show tune, and a little girl was twirling to the music. A faint chill was in the air, which reminded Omeer that yet another fall was coming. He waited for his Samoan to see him, wondering if she would notice his hair. When she did finally look, he held up his plastic container of mango like a prize to show her, and she smiled and held her container of mango up too, like a toast. He purposefully did not look in her direction again, so that she would know he was not trying to be intrusive, filled with reined-in joy as he was.

Omeer was working the door when his son came in that evening. The boy was carrying his saxophone case in one hand, said, "Hi," and lingered. The lobby was quiet and the sun was still up, but weakly.

"How was camp today?" Omeer asked.

"Ok," the boy said, not looking at him.

"Would you like to eat your dinner down here behind the desk with me?" He hadn't asked him to do that since the slap, over a month ago. He hadn't apologized either, although he was beside himself with complicated regret.

"Ok," said the boy, "but I have to practice first," and it was agreed that he'd bring his plate down with him after practicing and they would sit together, hidden behind the marble front desk while the boy ate.

"Have you ever tasted mango?" his father asked him when he came down. It was dark outside now, and the boy said he hadn't. "I have some left over from my lunch. It's lovely."

The boy took a bite and closed his eyes. "It tastes like a pine tree," he said, and his father was proud of him for that. It sounded like poetry to Omeer, like something a smart boy would say.

There were people coming and going, and Omeer had to get up several times to let them in or out. He turned the little TV on for the boy to watch, with the sound turned way down, but the boy turned it off again and read his book that he had carried down under his dinner plate.

When Omeer sat down again, the boy said, "You look different," and smiled a little at his father. Omeer remembered with shame slapping the boy's soft, round cheek.

He said to the boy, "Don't worry about me, ok? Soon you will be better than I am, and remember that I want that for you. I want you to be better than me." He looked at his boy, at his shiny black hair, at his face turned up to Omeer. "You mustn't feel bad when you surpass me." The boy might not understand now, thought Omeer, but he'd remember and understand later, maybe. The boy shrugged and, folding down the page of his book, turned the TV on so that a picture sprang up. "I look different to you?" Omeer asked him.

"Your eyes or something," the boy said, staring at the TV screen. He turned to look at his father for a moment. "Your eyes don't look so tired." He turned back to the television.

A woman in a large hat came to the door and asked to be announced to Mrs. Jacobs on the seventh floor, but Mrs. Jacobs didn't answer Omeer's call.

"Jesus Christ," the woman in the hat said, sighing deeply and staring off above Omeer's head. "So now what am I supposed to do?"

"I'm terribly sorry," said Omeer, aware that he was apologizing to this woman who meant nothing to him and that he had not apologized to his son. He felt the boy watching and wondered how his boy would come, finally, to think about his father.

"I am truly sorry," Omeer said to the woman. He bowed a little to show how sorry he was, but still she looked angry and wasn't turning to leave.

She seemed like tangible evidence that his currency was continuing its devaluative slide. Omeer had failed his wife, had slapped his son, had gotten himself in debt for nothing, and now he stood apologizing to strangers. His wife only smiled at him in her sleep now, and he was not allowed to share her bed anymore.

Mrs. Jacobs from the seventh floor came in the front door finally and calmed the woman with the hat down, leading her out into the park. He could hear the woman in the hat say, "Jesus Christ," and he heard Mrs. Jacobs say, "It's not his fault, Mary! God!" She rolled her eyes conspiratorially over her shoulder at Omeer, and he smiled, relieved.

The boy pretended to be watching TV, but Omeer knew he had witnessed the small disturbance and his father's ineffectiveness.

"What a lucky man I am," Omeer said, tears standing up in his eyes. This was as close as he could come to saying that he was sorry, for the slap, the debt, his position in the world, for being unloved by the boy's mother. He put his hand on the boy's shoulder, and the boy allowed it to stay there a moment before shrugging it off.

The piano music continued into the fall. The woman with the purses wrapped in Saran Wrap continued to come every Tuesday, and Omeer wondered where she would go for the winter. Who would understand that, although once her shoes had been on the wrong foot, she deserved a place to sit on a Tuesday afternoon to feel like she was not alone?

His Samoan came only once in September and she was with a friend, a co-worker maybe. Omeer was so happy to see her that he jumped up without thinking and tipped his little folding chair over. He righted it and fled the park, his face warm, tremendously glad to have seen her.

He saw her for the last time in October when she showed up for the final piano performance of the year. She had on a long sweater that came below her knees over her tangerine-colored Spandex outfit. She was pushing a wheelchair with an old man in it. The man was unmoving and listing sharply to one side. The Samoan's robustness and polish made the man in the wheelchair look chalky and frail like a dried white leaf.

She sat down in a chair just a few tables over from Omeer, and he could hear her talking softly to the man. She took care of him, Omeer realized. This was her job. The pianist came out, a jacket on against the chilly October afternoon. It was a Tuesday, Omeer knew, because the Saran Wrap lady was there, placing her purses on chairs like she was having a tea party and each purse was a guest. His Samoan pulled a sleeve of Oreos from her purse and put one in the old man's hand, pushing his fingers together so he wouldn't drop it. She whispered loudly in his ear, "It's a cookie. You can eat it."

She stood up behind him and patted down his hair with her colossal hand very gently, smiling down on him. The music started. It was classical, gorgeous, complicated music. It felt like a party. For a moment Omeer enjoyed his place in the park and forgot his debt, the way he embarrassed his son, his wife's dismissiveness, the board president's complaints. He felt these people in the park, the man pushing the garbage can and catching every fallen leaf, the woman with the wrapped purses, these were his friends too or, if not his friends exactly, well, they shared something.

His Samoan was tapping on the old man's shoulder, swaying to the music. Omeer could see her enormous rounded calves like half-melons beneath her long sweater. He could see his building just beyond her, and a wedding party emerging from the hotel next door to it. They served coffee there for $9 a cup. He had asked the hotel's doorman. Nine dollars a cup. Imagine that, and people paid it.

The two men who had cleaned out the coins from the fountain earlier were there, whispering to each other, their heads close together, laughing, leaning on their brooms. The wind was in the piano player's hair and made his smile look like it hung under a white cloud. There was a mother with her child asleep in its stroller, completely limp, while the mother texted on her phone to someone who was far away.

Omeer thought of those people in the paper who had lowered the park decades before. They had been visionaries. They had. As everything fell away, his savings, his marriage, his hair, Omeer knew he was still tremendously lucky. Lowering the park had, despite reason and cost and common sense, made the park into a palace, Omeer's palace. Here he sat amidst the swirling leaves, knowing that he would be back in spring, right here to listen to the music with his companions, the park like a cradle, rocking them all together. Incredible.

# Sky View Haven

Dad at eighty-five was pretty far gone already, even before he fell down the stairs with such vigor that he ripped the banister right out of the floor. He lay at the bottom of the stairs while Mom tried to talk him into letting her call an ambulance. "What for?" he asked her. "Let's just lie here a while, shall we?" He loved spending time with my mother.

She called me from the emergency room. I could hear Dad in the background singing something operatic, Gilbert and Sullivan maybe. "Can you hear him?" she asked. "They gave him some joy juice and he's singing his heart out."

I heard a nurse say to my mother, "He has a nice voice."

And Mom replied, "Yes, well, he was an announcer, you know, on the radio." I could picture him in his hospital gown, with one arm in the air for dramatic effect.

"He's fine mostly," she said to me, "he just can't stand on his own, so they're sending him to a nursing home for a few days, to Sky View Haven for rehab."

"How are you?" I asked Mom, who was eighty herself and skinny as a sparrow.

"I'm fine," she said, "I wish they'd give *me* some joy juice. Oh, one other thing. They've screwed up his meds and he's hallucinating just the tiniest bit."

35

"He's hallucinating?"

She paused, sniffled a little and lowered her voice. "He thinks I'm a Nazi," she said.

Dad was singing loudly in the background, then stopped.

Mom said, "Hold on," and put her hand over the phone. I heard her say, "Well, that's not very nice."

Then I heard him say, "You're right, of course you're right. I know you're not."

"He just apologized," she said to me, "for calling me a Nazi again, but listen, you have to visit him this weekend, starting Friday. He's very disoriented and I'm out of town with Aunt Flo for her hysterectomy." Dad said something I couldn't hear and Mom snapped at him, "Oh for Christ's sake, I am NOT." Then to me she added, "Friday, Saturday and Sunday, ok? Stay at our house so you don't have that long drive."

• • • •

I left home late enough to miss rush hour traffic over the Tappan Zee Bridge, stopping for a pedicure to kill time. I handed the girl a bottle of Jelly Apple Red polish as though I were headed for a beach vacation instead of to a nursing home. Grabbing a stack of *People* magazines, I fell asleep in the massage chair without reading them while she did my toes.

At my parents' house, I dropped off my bags and picked up the copy of Dr. *Jekyll and Mr. Hyde* that Dad and I had been reading. Dad used to read to me at night before bed, but my childhood ritual had flipped. Dad couldn't read to himself anymore, could hardly hold a book or focus his eyes, so I read to him, looking up often to see if he understood, to see if he was still awake. As he was already diminished before the fall, I didn't know what to expect now that he was in a nursing home hallucinating. How much worse could he be?

Sky View Haven, a nursing home for the well-heeled of Westchester County, sits perched on a cliff overlooking the Hudson River, a precarious spot, I thought, for old people who tend to

36

fall off things regularly and with gusto. In the lobby they had a floor-to-ceiling birdcage filled with a dozen Rainbow Finches the pastel colors of Jordan almonds. They preened and perched and feathered their tiny nests while I waited for the elevator, trying not to make eye contact with the woman standing next to me who smelled of Lysol. I tapped on the glass of the cage and noticed how full their food bowls were, how the bottom of their cage was covered with empty seed hulls. It was a plentiful, if trapped, life they led. Up on the fifth floor, the doors opened onto a panoramic view of the Hudson becoming more distinct as the sun rose above the pale blue hills and burned away the haze.

Next to the elevator was a woman in a wheelchair. Her face came to a point at the tip of her nose and she held a stuffed dog with large, floppy ears. She petted it and whispered to it, her lips moving silently. She had on a bright red sweatshirt with a reindeer on the front. I said, "Hello," which caused her to whisper furiously to her stuffed dog, and then rub his ears to calm him down.

When I got to Dad's room, he was agitated. "You're here, thank God. They were supposed to take me to the nursing home."

"You're here, Dad. You're in the nursing home." A little green teddy bear sat on his nightstand wrapped in cellophane. It had a festive Mylar balloon tied to its paw, which read, "Welcome to Sky View Haven" followed by an exclamation point that seemed to gild the lily.

"No," he said, "they were supposed to take me to the nursing home." He was staring into the middle distance, and I sat down on the edge of the bed and patted his leg. His fingers moved across the top of the sheet, back and forth like he was playing the piano. "They don't know what they're doing. I was supposed to go to the nursing home." His forehead felt warm to me and his toes, which stuck out from the bottom of the sheet, looked bony and enormously vulnerable.

I tried to get him to understand and finally just said, "We're going to the nursing home later," and he calmed down.

"You're mother's a Nazi," he said, finally, shaking his head in disgust.

"I heard."

"And there is a Croat following me." He pronounced it Kro-At.

"A Croat?" I asked, surprised.

"A *dirty* Croat," he said, emphasizing the word "dirty."

"Duly noted," I said. We sat there for a while, him silently worrying about his Croat, me wondering when he had developed a disdain for Croatian people. I tried to open the window for some fresh air, but it had been soldered shut.

A little later the aide lifted Dad into a wheelchair, and I rolled him down the hall to the common area, where the giant TV was blaring the local weather. Dad suddenly froze and grabbed my hand. "That's him," he said out of the side of his mouth, too loud as always. "That's the dirty Croat." He pointed with his elbow at a guy in a wheelchair who was propelling himself around the room using his feet. The guy spotted us and hurtled our way. Dad squeezed my hand.

"This," the Croat said, pointing at my dad, "is a wonderful man." My dad refused to even look in his direction. "Is he your father?" he asked me, his accent thick. I nodded. "Your father is a great man," he said, smiling broadly so that the wide spaces between every single tooth in his mouth were visible.

Dad whispered loudly and with great indignation, "Take me back to my room right now." As soon as we got into the hallway, he said, "He's not even supposed to be here. Did you see that? Did you?"

"I sure did see that," I said, hoping the bad meds would leach away soon. I wanted a normal conversation with my father.

That evening, after the aide got Dad into his pajamas, we read a few pages of *Dr. Jekyll and Mr. Hyde*. Dad began to snore softly and I put the book down. "Don't stop," he whispered, half asleep. "How will they know where to find me?"

"How will *who* know where to find you?" I pushed a wisp of white hair off of his forehead but he just asked the same question again. "I'll tell them where you are," I said, "I'll leave them a note." He used to leave notes by my bed when he came home too late to read to me. They said things like, "I was here but didn't want to wake you."

He began to snore again, and I whispered, "Dad?" I felt all roiled up and rotten, filled with regret over everything on earth. I wanted to say something to him, but didn't know what, so I gripped the rail on the bottom of the bed and whispered as quietly as possible, so as not to wake him, "I'm sorry."

"You should be," he said, his eyes closed, his snoring resuming again almost immediately.

The woman in the red sweatshirt with the reindeer on it was still by the elevator when I left. She was eating ice cream with a little plastic spoon and trying to feed it to her stuffed dog. I told her, "Good night," and she leaned over to whisper to her dog, keeping an eye on me.

Back at my mother's house, I showered for almost an hour, watching the soapy water swirl around my Jelly Apple Red toenails.

There was leftover Chinese in the fridge, which I ate in my pajamas, my hair wet from the shower. I tried to parse why I felt so awful, besides the obvious. There was a lot I hadn't accomplished, and it sickened me to think of it. I put my fork down. He would never know if I finally had kids, for instance. He'd be left with this unfinished version of me that I hoped, one day, might be so much more.

•  •  •  •

On Saturday, I got to Sky View in time for lunch. All of the patients had been wheeled into the TV room. They had bibs around their necks, and CNN was on so loudly that no one even tried to talk. Nurses in candy-colored scrubs, the shades of the Rainbow Finches in the lobby, flitted around the room, cheerfully doling out medication. The sun poured in the window and reflected brightly off of the river below. I stood in the doorway, and watched. The patients looked like white-haired birds, perched in their wheelchairs, their mouths wide open, waiting for food and pills to be dropped in.

I spotted the dirty Croat across the room and we waved at each other. The lady with the dog was in red again, and sat at one of the tables moving her lips silently. As I walked past, she grabbed my sleeve. I looked down and she was grinning at my red coat. "Hello," I said. She let go and leaned over her lunch tray to whisper something to her milk carton.

"Thank God you're here," my dad said. "They're giving me the wrong food. I specifically signed up for chicken and mashed potatoes." He pointed at the tray in front of him with disgust. "This is all wrong."

"It looks like chicken and mashed potatoes to me, Dad."

"It's the wrong order," he insisted so I picked up the tray and carried it over to the nurse's station and said hello to the woman in pink who was standing there. I read her name tag.

"Hi Janice," I said, "I'm pretending to get my father a different meal."

"Gotcha," she said, winking at me.

I waited a minute and then brought the tray back to Dad. "Here's the right meal," I said. "It's all straightened out."

"Thank God you're here," he said, and dug in. I pulled over a chair and tried not to take in the calamity of him eating, his extended tongue, the worn-down, yellowed cores of his teeth, the food falling in thick, gelatinous drops on his terry cloth bib.

"Where's Mom?" he asked.

"She's with Aunt Flo for the weekend," I said, "Remember? Aunt Flo's getting a hysterectomy?"

Dad looked confused. "Is Mom ever coming back?" he asked, with a sudden, deep sadness in his eyes. He put his fork down, waiting to hear.

"Yes," I said, "Mom's coming back." God, his love for her was intense.

"How will she know where to find me?" He reached for my hand and I thought he was going to cry.

"I'll tell her where you are." I said. "I'll leave her a note."

"I thought she was a Nazi," he said, "I have to apologize." He began to eat again.

"That would be nice, but she isn't mad."

"Yes, but I think I called her a Nazi."

"You probably should apologize then, when she gets back."

We went to his room after lunch and the aide kicked me out so she could bathe Dad. I visited the Rainbow Finches in the lobby and tapped on the side of their enormous cage again. How could you tell if a bird was happy?

Then I meandered through the cafeteria full of bibbed, leaning strangers, and out to a large veranda that looked down through the trees and onto the wide, gray river. Three people on separate benches were smoking. I leaned over the brick wall and looked at the water flowing past. It was cold and sunny, and spring was arriving. The local paper said that there were bald eagles up on this part of the river, but I didn't see any. One of the smokers was an angry looking old woman with thin, tightly curled white hair. As I walked past her she said, "Go fuck yourself."

And I said, "I know exactly how you feel."

•  •  •  •

When I arrived at Dad's room on Sunday, he announced, "They're having a cocktail party later. Wine and cheese." He paused, "But how will they know where to find me for the party?"

"Well Dad," I sighed, "they know you're in Room 501, so they'll probably look for you here."

At three they came for us. Dad seemed to be emerging a little from the hallucinations and he was very excited about the cheese. We made our way to the TV room, which was packed with weekend visitors. A nurse with a gigantic and animated rear-end was lumbering from patient to patient. "Red wine or white?" she spoke loudly into the face of an inert man strapped into his wheel chair. An orderly was handing out Styrofoam plates of cubed cheese and everyone, the employees anyway, were acting festive.

I got Dad set up with his back to the window and pulled a chair next to him. We watched everyone get served and when the orderly handed us our plate of cheese, Dad said, imperiously I thought,

"Take it back. I want more cheese." I felt I should apologize, but the orderly didn't seem flustered. He came back with a heap of white and orange cheese cubes on the plate. Dad smiled at me. I could tell he really felt he was getting his money's worth.

A nurse wheeled the lady in red to a table. She didn't have any visitors with her, but someone had put an enormous red bow in her hair for the party, making her head look small and pointy, revealing the little girl she had once been who was now trapped in this crone's body. The nurse handed us each a cup with an inch of wine in the bottom. Dad and I clicked ours together and said, "Cheers!"

The dirty Croat wheeled up next to me and said hello. Out of the corner of my eye I saw Dad purposefully turn his head away. "Hello," I shouted over the TV. "So, you're from Croatia!"

"No," he said, "I'm from Rome."

"Really? You're not from Croatia?" Perhaps he was mistaken.

"I'm from Rome," he said. "Your father, he is a great man."

"He's alright," I said, shrugging. Great wasn't the word that came to mind at the moment.

"No. No, he is a great man. I was a pianist in Rome, a professional pianist, and when I moved to America, I listened to him every afternoon on the radio for twenty years. I learned my English from listening to his show! He is a great man."

"Oh," I said. "Right." I was finding it hard to remember who Dad had been before all of this, before old age had begun to pluck his identity away. I thought about what I had known to be true about him. He had been on the radio. He had read to me at night. He had played jazz trombone, had told raucous dirty jokes, spoke Italian to waiters. But the actual memories of him were slipping away from me. This list of what I remembered seemed to be about someone else entirely. The person in front of me now, hoarding his processed cheese cubes, was the only father I could imagine anymore.

"He's a great man, your father," the man from Rome repeated, spitting as he talked so that bits of cheese flew through the spaces between his teeth and into my cup of wine.

We were interrupted by the lady in red, who began sobbing loudly. She was holding her dog very hard around the neck like she was holding on for dear life.

"For your dog," I said, going up to her and holding out a little red napkin I'd found at my mother's house. "I thought you could tie it around his neck like a scarf." She looked up at me, her mouth wide open, paused mid-sob. Her scalp was visible under the big red bow. She whispered something to the dog out of the side of her mouth, and then snatched the napkin from my hand like a thief.

When I got back to Dad, he wanted to know why I had been speaking to the Croatian guy. "Get this!" I said, "He's not Croatian! He's from Rome, and he used to listen to you on the radio."

"He's a fan?" Dad asked, straightening up a little in his wheelchair, posing.

"Yes, I suppose he is. He's a fan."

"He's Italian?" Dad had been fluent in Italian, had been to Venice and Rome. He loved Italy, loved Italian people. "So," Dad said, "he's a dirty Italian."

"Yes," I said, "exactly."

• • • •

When it was time for bed, I read the last few pages of *Dr. Jekyll and Mr. Hyde* out loud. Dad seemed perfectly lucid as I closed the book.

"So Mr. Hyde," he said, "never turns back to Dr. Jekyll in the end, I guess. Is that what we're supposed to understand?"

"Yes, that's right."

"So he's just a monster then, forever?"

"Not a very happy ending," I admitted.

"Yes, well. Robert Louis Stevenson certainly is a depressing fellow." We sat there for a while thinking about the book, as the room darkened around us.

"Mom's coming back tomorrow," I told him.

"How will she know where to find me?" he asked.

"Nazis have a great sense of direction," I said.

He laughed, which was a relief. "I have to remember to apologize to her about that."

"She isn't mad, but it's probably a good idea anyway. Dad?" I said, standing at the foot of his bed, shifting from one foot to the other. I looked down at my hands. "I don't know, I just wanted to tell you that I'm sorry."

"For what?"

I couldn't look at him. "I don't know. For you being here. For fighting with you so much. For never having kids. You know. I'm just sorry for everything."

He smiled and shook his head. "You should be," he said. "I know I am." We looked out the window together at the wide river just a shade lighter than the sky now. Dad turned to me and said quietly, "Some people died in the park." He leaned forward from his bed to tell me, as though it were urgent news, his eyebrows knit together in concern.

"What park?"

"Bryant Park, just outside of my apartment." He used to have an apartment there on Fortieth Street in New York City.

"How did they die?" I asked, confused about whether this was a real story he'd seen on TV or something he'd hallucinated.

"There was a tsunami," he said, his eyes enormous and sad, "and all of the people watching the Monday night movie in the park got washed away." He looked so crushed by the news that I just sat down on the edge of his bed. We sat like that, quiet for a while, together.

I finally said, "It must be awful to be washed away by a tsunami."

"Believe me," he said shaking his head, "it is."

• • • •

As Dad was falling asleep, I peeked into the hallway. The woman in red was still next to the elevator. She had tied the napkin I gave her around the dog's neck. She touched her nose to his and looked tenderly into his plastic eyes before tucking him into her lap for

44

the night. I left a note for Dad on his bedside table. "Mom will see you for breakfast." I was going to leave it at that, but added, after a moment, "I gave her your room number so she'll know where to find you."

# Milagro

Benny had never been a talker, not ever, and when his teeth started to go bad in his forties, whatever talking he had done before slowed from a trickle to a dried-up river bed. His wife pushed him. "Talk to your boss," she said, "maybe he'll help pay for the dentist." Sure enough he managed to get a whole new set of teeth without saying too much. To his wife's dismay though, he was embarrassed by the teeth, which he found too white and large for his face, so he wouldn't even open his mouth. She left Benny, and when she did, well, what was left to say?

He never spoke about his wife leaving, but the neighborhood had known her complaints. "He just sits there. Jesus," he'd heard her tell Belinda and Remo. "The silence drives me crazy, makes my ears ring." He had tried but the sound of his own voice seemed jarring and irrelevant to his ears. He held her hand, though, and sat next to her on the couch when they watched TV. He tried to make up for his silence with the noise of his closeness, but it wasn't enough.

When she left, it felt like the natural conclusion to their story. Part of Benny was relieved. Being incapable of making her happy had worn his heart down, like she had been an empty glass he'd been unable to fill, the never-being-enoughness of their relationship had exhausted him. On the other hand, he missed the sound

47

of her chatter. At night, in bed, he used to roll over and go to sleep, listening to the sounds of her whispers against his back, telling him everything that had happened that day.

Now he had to learn to fall asleep in silence, with no one whispering to him in the dark. Watching *Jeopardy!* seemed hollow now without her cursing out Alex Trebek. "Oh would he just shut up?" she'd say to the television. He had loved that, the way she had a comment for everything.

A few years after she left, his neighbors up in the Bronx began referring to him as a widower, and Benny didn't bother to correct them. What he said, or didn't say, didn't change much. He was okay with that.

With her departure, a quiet settled over his apartment like a fine dust. Nothing was ever interrupted without her there, and so he settled into a routine, and that routine had a kind of comfort of its own. He showered every morning using Irish Spring soap while his coffee boiled on the stove. The combination of smells—the tang from the soap, the warm mud of the boiling coffee—snapped the apartment back into focus every morning, gave it a feeling of intent. Benny stood in front of the fogged bathroom mirror, one of the green towels his wife had picked up at Macy's tied around his thin waste. He squeezed green gel onto his hands and rubbed it through his long, salt-and-pepper hair. Then he brushed his hair back into a low ponytail using a band that he kept in the little depression on the sink meant for soap.

No matter the weather, after his shower, he pulled up the shade on the kitchen window to let the day flood in as he drank his coffee, black, bitter. He ate his buttered toast dipped in the coffee to soften it. Even with his new teeth he preferred his food soft, liked the way the butter swirled into the coffee in an iridescent spiral. He liked the way the sun invaded his apartment, the way the butter changed the coffee.

Then he'd get dressed for his job in the park downtown. He washed his big glasses every morning and put them on. They got dark in the sunlight, just how he liked it. There was one drawer just for work clothes; he'd accumulated five green summer shirts and two pairs of summer work pants. He'd had three but got a tear in the seat of one on the subway home one night. He fixed the pants, sewed them up himself with small, even stitches, but he'd never worn them again. He was neither the kind of man to wear patched clothes, nor to throw away pants.

Working in the park Benny was outdoors all day, even in winter, even in the rain, and he never needed to speak. He was given a garbage can on wheels, a dustpan with a long handle and a yellow plastic broom, his own broom that no one else used. He knew no one else used it because he took the broom home with him, even though he wasn't supposed to. It was worn just right, so that on one side it was flat and could sweep up piles of leaves, while on the other it was worn to a point, so that Benny could get stubborn leaves out of the cracks between the stones. His instructions were to keep moving, to maintain a professional presence in the park, to keep it looking tended.

One guy who worked on the planters told him, "Benny, man, slow down why don't you? You make the rest of us look bad." Benny knew that it was not talking that saved him so much time. So he shrugged and kept sweeping, moving in his slow but focused circle around the fountain, getting every leaf and scrap of paper that was there, taking pleasure in the one moment when the square in front of him was leaf-free before moving on, knowing that over his shoulder another leaf was swirling down to the ground, that some tourist was dropping a candy wrapper. Benny kept moving. Benny didn't look back.

His morning routine was the same on the weekends only he didn't go to work after the boiled coffee and the shade being pulled up. In winter he went to the senior center and played cards. The rest of the time, in spring, summer and fall, he went to the community garden, putting a folding chair into his red shopping cart along with a Thermos of hot black coffee and a sleeve of paper cups. Remo, who was married to Belinda, brought a white box of cookies from the bakery. Jojo brought the cards, and Remo, Jojo and Benny, and maybe a fourth if the old man showed up, would sit playing cards, watching the kids work in the garden, listening to the women chatter and laugh like a flock of gulls, sometimes instructing, sometimes scolding the children. Lunch was brought either by Belinda or they'd go get a nice loaf of bread from the same bakery as the cookies, and then chip in for cheese or ham to share around. Benny studied his cards and listened to everything. He avoided the hard bread because of his teeth, but the cheese was ok with him, or a cookie, if it was the soft kind.

• • • •

One spring day when the chill was just wearing off—late May maybe—Belinda came up to the card table by the garden, put her hand on her husband Remo's shoulder and said, "Our stupid daughter gave her kid a baby chicken." So maybe it was around Easter that year.

"So?" asked Remo. "So what are you telling *them* for?"

"We can't keep it," said Belinda, tugging at the overburdened bra strap across her back. "Turns out they're all allergic or something, and you know her husband, if he's unhappy they're all unhappy." She paused. "He's not happy . . . about the chicken. And us, we've got the dog." She pointed down at Mitzvah, her little terrier mutt on its leash at Belinda's feet.

Remo started to deal. "Stupid dog," he said and the dog jumped his little front paws onto Remo's knee, which he pushed off, but gently. "Stupid dog," he whispered with a smile. It was the morning still. It was cold enough out that a little puff of smoke rose when Benny opened the Thermos. No one else said anything about the chicken. Belinda shrugged and went back to the garden where the school kids were being shown how to turn over the dirt in one of the little flowerbeds, getting the dirt ready to be planted.

After lunch, there the four men were, still at their table. It was a bread and ham day, so Benny wasn't eating but chewing on a toothpick. Someone, Remo maybe, had brought a radio that was set on the sports station and Benny was listening. Belinda came up to the table, picked up the loaf and broke a piece of bread off. Benny said, without looking up from his cards, "I'll take her." They were all startled enough to hear him speak that no one wanted to make the poor man clarify. He saw the looks on their faces and smiled so broadly that everyone saw his new teeth for the first time, and smiled with him, shocked by how white they were, and how uniform. "The chicken," he said. "I'll take her." He couldn't stop smiling, but managed to do it with his mouth closed so as not to draw attention to himself.

"But you don't have no yard or anything," Remo said, and Benny just waved him off with one hand and looked over his cards.

Belinda brought the chicken by to Benny's apartment a week later in a cardboard box that had once held paper towels. "I don't know how you plan on handling this," she said, putting the box on the floor in the kitchen. "You want her in the bathroom maybe?" Belinda was down on the floor with the box and looked up at Benny, who shook his head. Benny had gone to the library and looked up what a chicken might need to be happy. He had gotten chicken feed and put it in an old garbage can, and had a little Tupperware container of gravel for her too, which was supposed to be good for something called her "crop." He'd spread out a few old copies of the *Daily News* in the corner of the kitchen near the window. "You got a place for her to roost?" Belinda asked. "She needs to go up on something sort of high at night, you know, to roost on, or whatever. That's what my daughter says."

Benny waved for Belinda to follow him into his bedroom. He slid open the closet door that had belonged to his wife. It was empty, not a hanger on the pole, not a shoe on the floor. He had lined the bottom with newspaper, and because he didn't know how well the chicken would be able to fly up to her roost where his wife's clothes had once hung, he'd set up milk crates, one on top of the other, so she could hop up if she wanted to. "Her name's Cluck," said Belinda. Benny shook his head *no*. "Looks like you got everything set up, but if you need help with her or something, not that I know what to do with a chicken, except fry one up," she

51

laughed, "just kidding. But you know, let me know if you need anything. Hey, wanna look at her before I go? Just make sure she's ok from the walk over?"

They went back to the kitchen. "She not that old, not full grown yet. You'll see. She won't lay eggs for a little. Ok Cluck, here we come." Benny pulled the shade down and turned off the overhead light. She'd been in the box for a few blocks and he didn't want to dazzle her with all the daylight in the kitchen. Belinda opened up the box and Benny leaned way over, peering in. He could see a dark shadow in the corner, and could smell the cedar chips the chicken must have been in at Belinda's daughter's house. He heard her faint whine and crackle, and when Belinda stood back, the chicken hopped up onto the rim of the box.

She was black and glossy and a big girl for not being full-grown yet, nice and round, shaped like a teakettle. She had a red crown, and more red hung beneath her black beak as she turned her head from side to side.

Benny was glad when Belinda finally left. He'd planted a window box full of basil that he brought out of the bathroom. He thought maybe the chicken would like some dirt to peck in, and he had bought some worms from a friend who was a fisherman, and had put them in the dirt in the flower box where they had wriggled right down and hidden in the roots of the basil.

"Hello," he whispered to the chicken, and she turned her head so that one of her eyes was looking right up at him. "In the meantime," he let the sentence trail off and put down a metal pan with the corn meal and a few pieces of gravel for her crop on the newspaper, and then he put down a bowl of water, and after that he put the flower box down on the newspaper too, but in a spot where, once he lifted the shade again, a beam of sunlight shone on it to help the basil grow. He sat at the table listening to the chicken peck at her metal dish, her feet making a pleasant sound as they rattled the newspaper beneath. Benny looked around the kitchen, smiling again. Up on the shelf over the sink with the Fantastik, he saw the bottle of Milagro Tequila that had been his wife's, unopened since she'd left. "Milagro," he said. So that was her name. When he said it, it sounded soft and round, like her. Milagro.

On weekends, Benny perched Milagro on the handle of his red shopping cart and she rode with him to the garden. The kids loved her, but Benny was scared they'd be too rough with the hen, so he kept an eye out. Janice, a little girl with very curly hair who was bad already at six years old, threw a rock at Milagro. Benny stood over Janice, staring down at her through his enormous dark glasses, silent, his hand on her shoulder. He waited until she laughed a little. Then she shifted from one foot to another, and still he stood over her, casting his shadow over her. Once she started crying, Benny patted her head and walked away. After that, she left Milagro alone to scratch in the garden beds from eight in the morning until the men's afternoon card game was done. She kept other kids away from the chicken, like she was Milagro's bodyguard.

At night, Benny pulled the kitchen window shade down, dimmed the lights at 7 p.m. and ate his dinner in front of the TV while he listened to Milagro scramble up to her roost. By 7:30 or 8, he slid the closet door shut and she was in for the night. He lay in bed and listened to her adjust her feathers, or whine softly in her sleep. It filled up the air enough to let him sleep.

In the mornings he let her out when he woke up and she headed for her water and feed dishes. Benny put up the shade then, and took the window box from the kitchen table (where Milagro was not allowed) and put it on her newspapers to scratch in. When she occasionally flew up to the table making a big racket with her wings, Benny put her on his shoulder and she would sit there sometimes while he drank his coffee. Otherwise, she busied herself around the apartment. She knew that the water dripped in the bathtub, for instance, and she made that part of her rounds. He swept every morning now, but on Saturdays he changed all of the newspapers and mopped the floors. When it got a bit colder, toward the end of September when the kids were still working in the garden on the kale, lettuce, carrots and nasturtiums, Milagro would sometimes sit on Benny's knee or shoulder while he played cards, fussing and clucking until she settled down. All of her little noises filled Benny up, like he was effervescent. It made him want to touch her feathers, which, when looked at closely, were not black, really, but an iridescent rainbow of greens and purples, like the colors in the butter that floated on his morning coffee.

"You have a straight flush," Remo would say. "I can see it in her eyes." The guys laughed, and Benny smiled, keeping his eyes on his cards.

Belinda had not been looking well that whole spring, and by summer it had gotten worse. Benny had noticed dark half-moons under her eyes, and figured that by June she had lost five pounds. By July it was eight, and by August the light in her face had started to dim. He never said anything, but he brought her things: an extra cup to share his coffee. He brought her a folding chair, opened it next to him and when Belinda stopped by, Benny patted the chair and she sat down.

One Sunday morning in September she leaned over to Benny who kept his eyes on his cards but leaned toward her nonetheless. "It's Mitzvah," she said, pointing to the dog sitting by her ankle. "She's the one I'm worried about. Remo pretends to hate her, but the truth is, it's all too much for him right now. And you, you've got a way with animals." She paused. "I know, I know, dogs and chickens don't mix, but they seem ok with each other. Mitzvah's not a chaser." She had put her hand on Benny's shoulder. He reached up and put his hand on her hand. He turned and looked at Belinda and she looked back. He smiled a closed-mouth smile, and she smiled back. The deal was done.

Belinda and Remo came by the next week with Mitzvah on a leash and a giant bag of kibble along with his food and water dish. "I'll come by and walk him while you're at work, if you want to give me a key," said Remo. Benny nodded. "I don't hate Mitzvah, by the way, but he'll be happier here probably." He whispered, "She can't really walk him so much now."

"Will your chicken be alright with him, do you think?" asked Belinda. Benny shrugged. He reached down and unhooked the leash from Mitzvah's collar. The three of them stood and watched as Milagro eyed Mitzvah from her spread-out newspaper.

Benny sat in the chair near the chicken and said, "Good girl," which made Belinda and Remo (who gave each other a look) wonder how much he spoke behind closed doors. Milagro hopped onto Benny's knee, and then Benny held out his hand for Mitzvah, who trotted over and stood on his hind legs, his front legs resting on Benny's other knee. Mitzvah panted and smiled into Milagro's face, trying to get a bead on her, while Benny pet Milagro's feathers lightly, whispering, "There's my good girl. There's my good girl." She crouched a little, fluffing up her pin feathers, and then jumped, landing on Mitzvah's neck. Mitzvah dropped his paws onto the floor and stood there, giving the chicken a chance to turn around and hold onto his collar. Then he went and drank from the chicken's water dish. It would be all right.

Remo took Belinda's skinny little elbow in the palm of his left hand, and put his right hand, opened up, on the small of her back.

"I can't do your stairs anymore," said Belinda over her shoulder, leaning on Remo.

"I'll see you tomorrow," said Remo to Benny. It would be the last day at the garden for the season. The air was chilly now, even in the daytime, and the school kids had picked the green tomatoes off of the stalks and given them to their parents to fry up. Then they had pulled up the dead tomato plants, and the roots of everything else, even the plants that still had buds on them. The garden had to be cleaned and mulched for the winter and so everything had to be ripped out and put in the compost pile. This was a good lesson for the kids, Belinda had told Benny, that everything dies and has to be cleaned up, so that in the spring it can come back. The garden was full of good lessons for the kids, she said.

At work in Bryant Park September was just like summer. The piano players still came every day at lunchtime, only it all felt sad, more like the memory of summer than like summer itself. There were loads of leaves to sweep, big piles, and Benny had to empty his garbage can several times a shift. And the guys who cleaned the fountain had to clean out the leaves twice a day, morning and afternoon, or the whole thing would get clogged up with leaves from the plane trees, which looked like maple tree leaves, only bigger and thicker.

• • • •

Belinda died early on a Tuesday morning in October, and Remo came by to tell Benny before Benny left for work. They sat at the kitchen table with Mitzvah in the corner, his head on his folded paws. "The dog knows," said Remo. "I can feel it. Belinda loved that stupid dog."

Benny nodded and dipped his toast in his coffee, but he didn't put it in his mouth. Instead, he put it back on his plate and put his hand over Remo's fist and left it there, like a blanket on a stone. Remo bent over till his forehead touched the Formica table, and Milagro clucked and fluttered up from the floor and landed on Remo's shoulder.

His head still on the table, Milagro on his shoulder eyeing Benny's toast, Remo said, "Can you get out of work tomorrow? Or go in late or something?" Benny had never missed a day of work, but he nodded, squeezing Remo's fist.

"Of course," he whispered.

Remo swiveled his head a little so that he could look up at Benny. "Would you be a pall bearer? I need pall bearers." Benny looked down at Remo and nodded. Of course he would. Of course.

Despite Remo's early morning visit, Benny still managed to get to work before the chains had been removed from the park entrances. Benny lowered his dark glasses and said to his supervisor, "I can't be here tomorrow." His supervisor, who was younger than Benny, and a lot taller, froze. Benny never spoke to him. In fact, he'd assumed Benny disliked him, the way he never smiled or hung out. He was already nodding "yes" when Benny added, "It's a funeral. I'm going to be a pall bearer."

"Jesus," said the supervisor. "Yeah, of course. No problem. Whatever." He put his hand on Benny's shoulder, sensing a chance to ingratiate himself. "Whatever, really." Benny pushed his dark glasses back up and nodded his thanks, as he walked over to the supply closet for his garbage can.

It was a beautiful day, sunny and clear, and the park filled up early. It was windy too, and with each gust a hundred leaves seemed to swirl down around him, like they were dancing. When Benny came up near the fountain, there was a guy in it, a guy all in black, a really sick guy Benny had seen before, a desperate guy, not well in his head, picking coins out of the water. Benny didn't stop, just stayed focused on the leaves, saw out of the corner of his eye the cop near the fountain texting. Benny stayed focused on the leaves. He got one spot clean, and then the next. More leaves would fall, but that was all right with him. The man in the fountain would fill his pockets and leave eventually. The cop would look up or he wouldn't. There would be music later at noon, and Benny would time it so that he could sweep there twice that hour, so he could hear the music two times at least.

When he got home, he got down the bottle of tequila he hadn't opened in ten years. He put the flower box on the floor for Milagro and pulled a Milk-Bone out of his jacket pocket for Mitzvah. He'd bought it on the way home. Then he sank into the kitchen chair. "To Belinda," he said, and drank a single shot down. He went to shower. He'd bring Mitzvah with him to Remo's later so that they could all sit shiva together.

Tomorrow would be the funeral and he'd be a pall bearer. He'd never done that before—figured he'd just see what to do by watching the other guys Remo had asked. His black suit and tie were still in the dry cleaning bag from the last funeral he'd been to back in winter. He'd help bury Belinda, and then the day after Belinda was buried, Benny would go back to work, back to sweeping up the leaves as they fell from the plane trees in the late summer (well, autumn technically) wind.

# Beautiful Mom

As I remember that night, the ice skaters wheeled around and around the Bryant Park skating rink like seagulls in a parking lot. There was tinny skating music piped through the thin night air, and the shops and rink in the park, which had probably looked festive a week ago, were needy and abandoned now that Christmas was over and New York City's post-holiday languor had set in. The bulkiness of my coat made my backpack keep slipping off my shoulder and down to my elbow.

We hadn't seen or even spoken to one another since she'd left us, what, two years ago? Dad had arranged for me to see Mom on my way back to school. It was important to them both, he assured me, but I knew he had set it all up. I waited at the foot of the Gertrude Stein statue where Mom and I were supposed to meet.

Stein, the poetess, sat on her marble pedestal watching over the park. I stared up at her sagging jowls, her bronze breasts that looked like fifty-pound weights. Ponderous and frank as Buddha, Gertrude sank into her seat of stone, plain as a brown paper bag. "A rose is a rose," my mother would have said. "A rose is a rose is a rose." She loved poetry, used to read to me at bed time, but I had pushed that out of my mind, another extinguished memory, or rather a memory I wished I could extinguish.

# The Subway Stops at BRYANT PARK

Anxious about my mother's arrival, I worried the eleven dollars in my pocket with my thumb. The time on my phone seemed to stop moving, so I folded my train ticket in half, and then unfolded it. Craning my neck around to catch sight of her entrance from whichever side of the park she chose, I shrugged the backpack up into its place. It fell down again.

I reached up and put my hand on Gertrude's cold knee and then I saw her, saw my mother. There was a faint click and hush as if the entire park slowed and silenced as she walked up the stone steps and made her entrance. Everything leaned toward her, as it always had. She was smiling and didn't see me, so I pulled back to draw out the not-being-seen, to enjoy her as she might look when she didn't know I was watching. Her straight, white-blond hair sparked as it brushed her shoulders. She smiled at a man without looking at him, and I could see her top lip settle back down over her teeth, which protruded just the right amount. Her long legs, in dark blue jeans, scissored as she walked, like the legs of a great blue heron. The coat she wore looked expensive, although I knew that if I wore it, it wouldn't. Her tiny leather purse, the bravado of wearing such high heels in the middle of winter, mesmerized me, and made me aware of the brownness of my hair, the thickness of the rubber soles on my sneakers, the dumb utility of my backpack, which slid down my arm all the way now and rested on the top of my foot. She was as breathtaking as ever. More maybe.

Then she saw me, peeking around Gertrude Stein's knee, and she waved. Coming out from behind the pedestal, I pulled my backpack up and pushed my shoulders back to stand up straight for her, to show her who I had become in her absence, not sure myself.

Mom put a soft, gloved hand on each of my cheeks and looked into my eyes. "My little girl," she cooed. I felt like I was in a movie, like I was the center of everything. She put her arm around my shoulder and whispered, "Suzie." I closed my eyes and imagined that the skaters and tourists were looking at us. Breathed in the leather and lemon that reminded me of being tucked in at night, another memory I'd submerged.

"You look beautiful," she said, pulling off one glove and pushing my hair behind my ear, "You look so good to me," and I wanted to believe her, wanted to look good enough to make her stay. "I forgot to get cash before I left the apartment," she said, "but I must have a credit card here somewhere."

"I have eleven dollars," I said. "Do you want it?" I took it out of my coat pocket and pushed it toward her.

She laughed and pushed my hand back. She seldom accepted what people offered her, I remembered, as though she preferred more subtle, complicated transactions. "No, no! I don't want your money." She laughed and I knew I had made a misstep. "I didn't mean that. Never mind, I probably have a twenty in here some-where." She indicated the leather purse, which was just the right size to hold a small paperback and a tube of lipstick. She probably used a twenty-dollar bill as a bookmark. Mom stood back and swept her eyes up from my sneakers taking in the length of me. "Wow, you're almost as tall as I am." She put her arm through mine like we were best friends.

"I'm five nine," I said, un-slumping.

"Men love tall women," she said. "You should be a model, I'm not kidding." But she wasn't looking at me when she said it, so I didn't bother to disagree. She steered us away from Gertrude and in the front door of the Bryant Park Café. "Let's sit at the bar," she said, as she did the dance that she did at bars, or parent-teacher conferences for that matter (as I recalled in that moment). Upon entering a room, my mother took stock of who was nearby, and of who had taken stock of her, and who *might* take stock of her, before she chose where to sit. Tonight, it seemed, we would sit on the stools in the middle of the long, copper bar.

A single man in a sport coat to our left lifted his chin and smiled at us, while the two men in dark suits, bankers maybe, on the other side, did not acknowledge us yet. The man who had smiled had a menu in front of him, and when the bartender asked what he wanted to eat, the man looked at Mom and seemed em-barrassed.

He said, "Forget it. How about a scotch and soda," and I remembered then that men didn't like to eat in front of my mother, that this kind of beauty undid them. They seemed to lose interest in regular things when she was nearby, as though everything but Mom should please go away. The bartender put a bread basket in front of him anyway, and took the man's menu.

"What can I get for you ladies?" The bartender slid coasters in front of each of us, and appeared unaffected by my mother. She made a show of thinking, putting her forefinger to her top lip and tapping it there. She squinted up at the ceiling, and then she leaned a little bit over the bar and tossed her head, perhaps so that the bartender could smell the lemon in her hair. She continued to stall and I worried that he would become impatient, but he must have smelled her hair, because although the bar was full, and people were waving credit cards at him, he stopped shuffling and stood perfectly still, like he would wait there forever to take her order.

The man in the sport coat said, "Let me get you two a drink," to which my mother laughed and reached over me to touch him on the sleeve of his jacket.

"She's only sixteen," she told the man, pointing at me with her thumb, and I could see that he felt blessed by her beauty, as we all had so often. He looked relieved, like her hand on his sleeve had answered questions he hadn't yet asked. "I'll have a vodka martini, up, with a twist, and she can have, what," she asked, looking at me, "a ginger ale?" The bartender moved away from us reluctantly, to his bottles and ringing phones, to the ordinary stuff of his night.

The men in the suits must have noticed her finally, because the one with a full head of bushy gray hair leaned over my mother's shoulder and said, "Where are you girls from?" and my mother went into her Washington-Square-Park-by-way-of-Louisiana story while I sipped my ginger ale. The man with the hair leaned in to her, looking into her eyes in the way I hoped and feared a boy might look into mine someday. He said with a grin, his eyes examining her skin, "You should be a model." She turned and gave me a conspiratorial grin.

"She is a model," I said shyly, proudly. "She is! You've seen her, probably. She was on a billboard last summer, in Times Square, for Clairol."

She laughed and looked down at her fingers. "Now, now," she said, patting my hand lightly as if she were too modest to have me talking about her, but then she gave me a light squeeze that I took to mean, "Good girl."

We sat at the bar for a while. "How's your father?" She leaned into me.

"He's ok." I had to shout to be heard because it was loud in there.

"And school? How's school?"

I sunk into one-word answers and she turned away eventually. I had two ginger ales and my mother had a few martinis, which I guess the guy with the bread basket paid for. When I stood to go to the bathroom she told me to leave my bag and coat on the stool, "So no one will take your seat."

She held my face lightly in her cool hands. "Suzie," she said, "you won't listen to what people say, will you?" She paused and I smelled the lemon peel on her breath, or later I thought maybe it was the vermouth. "I love you, no matter what you think." I wanted to tell her that I wished she hadn't left. I wanted to ask how she could leave us like that, but I stood still. She touched her forehead to mine and I looked into her eyes, which I could see, from this close, had become bloodshot. I pulled back and her eyebrows dipped together in worry for just a second. "Don't listen," she said, smiling now, and at this distance I couldn't really see her eyes, just her wagging finger as I backed away.

When I returned from the bathroom, I stood for a moment looking out of the window of the restaurant at Gertrude. Even seeing her from the back like this, she remained aggressively plain, like a dare, slouching as all of fashionable New York City passed her. I felt such sudden love for her. Someone had placed a used coffee cup on the pedestal by Gertrude's hip, but even an old cup with lipstick on it couldn't detract from the atmosphere of sturdy solemnity around her.

# The Subway Stops at BRYANT PARK

At the bar I told my mother that it was time for me to go, that my train back to school would be leaving soon, that I had to walk over to Grand Central. "Is it time already?" she asked, picking up the wrist of the man with the hair and looking at his watch with some confusion. "I'll walk you out," she said, and held my coat up for me. Then the man with the hair took her coat from her and slipped it over her waiting hands, which dipped down and back like the wing tips of a sea bird.

She smiled in the general direction of the bartender and the man with the untouched bread basket, and the one with the hair, and the friend of the one with the hair, but she didn't say goodbye to anyone. She just smiled and walked away, and I imagined them, hours later, still sitting on their barstools, leaning toward the door she had exited through. By the statue, her eyebrows dipped together again like she was worried. I didn't want to hear whatever it was she was building up to, so I cut her off before she said anything. "Mom, I have to hurry or I'll miss my train."

"Try not to think too little of me," she said. She was smiling to cover up whatever she was actually feeling. I wanted her to say she was sorry, to acknowledge that we had been friends once, that she had done something terrible, to make me feel better somehow. "I should have called," she said, "but I wasn't ever going back. I didn't know how to tell you that." She looked torn up for a second, and then she hugged me and I hugged her back with only one arm because my stupid backpack was sliding down again. My mother never said goodbyes, and when the hug was over, she turned and walked down the steps, out of the park and away, causing a flutter, I imagined, as she walked along 40th Street.

I headed in the opposite direction, across the park to 42nd Street, walking quickly to get to Grand Central. I had told the truth about the train arriving soon, although I had neglected to mention that they left every half hour. As I walked, I felt in my coat pocket for the ticket. My eleven dollars was gone. I stopped and checked the other pocket, and then I checked my jeans and took off my backpack and unzipped every pocket looking for the

64

money, even though I knew by then that I wouldn't find it. I knew I could never tell Dad, who would just feel too terrible for me, and he wouldn't understand that I had offered it to her in the first place. I had wanted to give it to her, wanted to give her whatever she would accept from me. And I still had my train ticket, anyway.

# Lucky Cat

Tommy stood over a skillet of sizzling butter, rosemary and garlic while Suzie stood in the doorway watching, confused. She folded up her resume and stuffed it into the pocket of her down vest and forgot that she was the looking for a job.

Tommy waved the smoke toward his twitching, hairy nose. He was handsome and disgusting. His thick fingers and stubbled chin, the smells that hung in the air, the food subdued and about to be consumed—all of it felt so sexual. She was compelled and deeply uneasy, feeling a clench and pull just above her pelvic bone that had to be attraction. Her mind went all blurry so that her body could focus. That's what sex was, right? She hardly knew.

Tommy raised his eyes and Suzie could feel him sizing her up. She felt how small her boobs were under the down vest, how she lacked the ease of some girls, the way some could look beautiful by not caring, their hair shiny and thick. She wanted men to lean in to her, men just like this guy, not the kids she knew from high school, but actual men with profuse hair and butter in their beards. Could he tell by looking at her that she was only eighteen? Could he smell her fear and need?

He smiled at her, then back down at the plump, raw scallops on a metal dish in front of him. She was just tipping over a cliff that she wanted to fall off of. If she fell, she felt he could catch her in those catcher's mitt hands, or maybe he was the cliff she was standing on. She shrugged and regretted the underwear she'd chosen that morning. Cotton. White. Old. A little baggy. Shit.

He pressed the raw scallops, one at a time, into the butter so that they spit and sizzled. He turned one over and Suzie could see the crisp edges of a perfect sear, the flecks of brown butter across the scallops' white cheeks. The chef's grin, sweet and terrifying, hovered in the smoke, and pulled at Suzie like some kind of diabolical kite.

He took down two bowls, ladled stew into them and placed a single, perfect scallop in the middle, pouring a circle of cream around each scallop like a fence.

"Bouillabaisse," was the first word he said to her, handing her a bowl. Did he know who she was, that she was just a stranger looking for a waitress job? Did he think she was someone else? She smiled a little and then thought about how dorky she probably looked, and stopped smiling.

"Bouillabaisse," she whispered. The ceramic bowl felt warm like a bird just fallen from its nest. She could almost feel its heartbeat. Tommy wiped his hands on his apron. They took up their spoons and stood, staring at each other, bringing spoonful after spoonful, wordlessly to their mouths.

By the time she swallowed the last bite Suzie had been permanently seduced. She would work whatever hours he offered her, for whatever pay. She understood then that she was the kind of girl who would be loyal to guys who didn't care whether or not she was loyal. She'd known it all along, sort of, that she would not be able to make demands of him. The smear of something oily across his T-shirt, the crumb of butter she only just now noticed in the stubble by the joint of his lips that were smiling at her crookedly . . . she was done. He had finished her. Her legs were trembling.

As she filled out her W-4 form in his office, Tommy said, "There's no ingredient beneath contempt. A real chef can make the plainest thing sing like a truffle." He wiggled his eyebrows at her, causing her to blush and keep her head down over her paper-work.

• • • •

College was starting for Suzie in a couple of weeks. Because she needed money, she didn't mind being put on brunches at Q, even though they were exhausting. Lines of people stretched around the block. And brunch customers were needy, asking for extra butter and endless coffee refills. They demanded little cold pitchers of cream, and little warm pitchers of maple syrup. They would ask, "Is the orange juice fresh?" in a way that implied they were emo-tionally invested in the answer. Suzie memorized lists of exotic herbal teas to recite like a litany. "Lavender, peppermint, jasmine," she would intone, "Golden chrysanthemum, blood orange." What was she praying for?

By the end of brunch shifts, Suzie was sticky from artisanal jam. Her hair was sweated down. Her hands smelled of coffee grounds and wet rags. As the last customers filed out onto Hudson Street, their expensive coats from Barney's draped over their drowsy, su-per-skinny frames, she felt like slapping them all for making her feel so plain.

On weekend mornings she left her shared apartment (five of them in a 1-bedroom) while it was still dark. She watched a door-man near Bryant Park in full doorman regalia, hunting among the rain-soaked garbage bags, stabbing at rats with an improvised spear, while the rats danced just out of reach. At first it shocked her that there were rats even in swanky parts of New York city, but becoming a New Yorker meant accepting that there were rats everywhere, and that they danced in the pre-dawn, rain-soaked streets before tourists awoke. Suzie was proud that early morning rats no longer flustered her, except for the one time that the door-man actually hit one with his spear and she looked away.

Q sat amidst the cobblestones of TriBeca just below Canal. Every Saturday and Sunday that summer, Suzie went west from her apartment and past Bryant Park, then west some more across

# The Subway Stops at BRYANT PARK

Times Square, empty in a post-apocalyptic way on early week-end mornings, with litter blowing through the streets. She headed down and west, through Chinatown, where plastic Lucky Cats sat in every shop window, their left paws bobbing back and forth, promising prosperity to everyone, over and over again, offering a constant, factory-made benediction to the people and litter and vermin that shared the streets.

The probability that there were rats in Q's basement didn't worry Suzy (she was sure there were), nor did it stop beautiful people from swarming the place. All restaurants in New York City probably had rats, and movie stars weren't going to cook for themselves. Everyone must know, she thought, and they were just pretending that everything was ok, that nothing was lurking underground.

The customers in TriBeca were different from the ones in Bryant Park where she had worked bussing tables. There were no scrubbed-up tourists in TriBeca, no crowds on the sidewalk gawking. Here there were movie stars and models and bankers who lined up at Q for *huevos rancheros*, for the ten-inch-tall slices of carrot cake that fell over with a whipped cream *pouf* when the waitresses slid them onto plates.

Tommy told Suzie, "Ignore the stars. Treat them like everyone else or they'll stop coming here." It was easy for her to ignore them. She was focused elsewhere, on the just-about-to-be-ness of her life. She ignored, too, the giraffe-like models with enormous rings and bracelets like pieces of turquoise-studded armor. Tommy was right. Famous people liked to be ignored. They came back with their famous friends and their neglected children, and sipped Bloody Mary's garnished with pickled okra. They ran their beautiful fingers, manicured by strangers, along the empty plates that had once held apple pie. They sucked the sugar and butter off those fingertips while they made deals and looked at the nannies disdainfully when their own children made too much noise.

• • • •

They slept together once, Suzie and Tommy, right after he hired her, but she hadn't been able to hold his attention. It happened late one night after a dinner shift. They were the last two in the restaurant and Tommy pulled down the metal bars over the windows and locked them. Then he brought out a bottle of Jägermeister and poured them each half a coffee cup full. "Drink it like a shot," he told her, so they tipped their mugs back. Suzie marveled at the sugary mixture of licorice and tar. It felt brave, experimental. They walked to his apartment around the corner and up the three flights of stairs. He fumbled with the keys while she hovered in the no-man's land between giggles and sighs.

Her expectations about sex with Tommy (or anyone for that matter) were murky, but still it wasn't the way Suzie had imagined it would be. Tommy gently removed her glasses and held her face with both hands and smiled down into it like she was a poaching egg in softly boiling water. She chose to trust him. He was so gentle with eggs, pushing his calloused fingertips into their yolky-hearts to see if they were ready, his fingers barely leaving an imprint on them. Like a blind man, he could sense when they would ooze properly if pierced with a fork. Suzie gave herself over and he was kind, kinder than she'd expected. He was. Yes. He was kind to her.

After they slept together, she didn't know what to do, how to take their relationship from one thing to something else. She had hoped the sex would change things automatically, but when it became clear that she would have to do something to make it so, she knew she wouldn't be able to pull it off. She didn't even know what to try. Should she be bossy? Elusive? She felt like a used car salesman unable to close a deal, awkward and stupid and desperate.

When it was time for her to work with Tommy again after the sex, she stole some of her roommate's expensive conditioner, but Tommy treated her just like he always had, ignoring her for most of the shift, and then asking her to smoke with him afterwards. Their friendship absorbed the one time they slept together, and Suzie decided that friendship with Tommy was enough, was what she had wanted from him in the first place anyway, as though she had any say in the matter. Things just fell back to how they had been before.

• • • •

It was just after Christmas, 3 or 4 months after the bouillabaisse and the W-4 form and the sex, that Suzie and Tommy saw the rat. It was after a busy Sunday brunch, and Suzie's apron was full of crumpled dollar bills making it lumpy and unflattering. Every last bit of appeal had been wrung out of her, and her appeal, even in the best of times, was unreliable. Her glasses, which had a thumb-print of syrup on them, had slipped down her nose as she bent over a table, chewing her Trident gum, scrubbing at some spilled maple syrup.

Tommy came out of the kitchen, his apron caked with hollandaise. He poured himself a mug of coffee and came up behind Suzie, putting a hand on her waist. She shot upright as he whispered in her ear, "Come down to the basement and smoke with me." His breath on her neck, his hand on her waist, the way he stank of burnt coffee made Suzie want to ease back against him. She said, "Sure," like she was hardly interested and followed Tommy to the steep, rubber-coated stairs to the basement. None of the other wait-staff even looked up.

It smelled of Clorox and puddles down there. Tommy had turned over two white buckets, and they sat down on them, just sort of collapsing over their cigarettes. Suzie wasn't a smoker, really. She only smoked with Tommy, and only cigarettes she bummed from him. She didn't know how to inhale right and held a cigarette awkwardly, the way she might hold something unreliable.

"The new busboy," she said, trying to sound like she knew things, "He doesn't know what he's doing." Suzie pushed up her glasses and took the clip out of her hair. She wanted Tommy to notice, but she was embarrassed to toss her hair around the way she had seen pretty girls do. Finally, she just tucked it behind her ears and tried to act the way someone who didn't adore him would act.

"Suzie, Jesus," said Tommy, "did you see that new waitress? Did you see her tits? Holy mother of God." He laughed and blew smoke out of his nose in two thick streams. "What's her name?" he asked. "The one with the tits. What's her name?"

"I don't learn the names of new people until they've been here at least a week," Suzie reminded him.

"Did I hire her?" he asked, and without waiting for her to answer he said, "Well, good for me."

"Yes, you hired her," Suzie said, "and you're gross. Seriously. You're disgusting." She beamed at him.

"I know," he said. "But I'm right, right? She's unbelievable, right?" He laughed.

Suzie said, "I guess. And I'm sure she'd really be into you." She waved her cigarette at him in a sweeping motion to take in his overall appearance. "You've got ham on your face," she said. "Is that ham on your face?" She laughed and shook her head as though she didn't know what anyone could possibly see in him. He rubbed his chin, missing the ham. "Ham stuck on his face," she muttered, smiling, shaking her head.

They sat there smoking silently, staring into the middle distance, shifting their asses on the hard plastic buckets. Then all of a sudden Tommy leapt up and screamed, so loud and high-pitched that Suzie screamed too while Tommy jumped up on his overturned bucket and screamed into the hand that he clamped over his own mouth. He danced from foot to foot, still screaming through his hand, pointing across the room. Suzie turned to see what he was pointing at, and there it was, on a white pipe just above eye-level.

The rat.

He was the size of what, a loaf of bread? A runt piglet? He seemed unperturbed by Tommy's screams, the rat's tail curling around the pipe languidly for balance. Suzie could hear the rat's nails click on the pipe as he crawled toward the wall.

"Holy fuck," Tommy whispered. Suzie tossed her cigarette into a puddle where it sizzled. Tommy jumped down from his bucket and placed himself so that Suzie stood between him and the rat. He put his hands on her shoulders and she shrugged them off as the rat disappeared along the pipe and folded itself inside the wall, tail and all.

They ran up the stairs and into Tommy's office and whispered so that the rest of the brunch staff, who were filling the salt and pepper shakers, wouldn't hear. Tommy fumbled in his pocket for money. His hands were shaking. "What are you going to do?" she asked. Was he planning on getting a gun?

"I'm going to the pound," he whispered, leaning right into her face, "and I am getting us a fucking cougar."

She liked that he'd said "us," and got the pound's address online, writing it out for him and pushing it into the pocket of his T-shirt. She took a fresh piece of Trident from her apron and handed it to Tommy. "Wait for me here, will you?" he asked. She smiled and nodded, shy and glad.

"I'll wait," she said, getting out a piece of gum for herself. She wondered if a cat would even dare to take on a rat the size of a piglet.

Suzie and Tommy walked nonchalantly through the dining room to the street. The waitress with the tits was doing her cash report and didn't look up as they passed. Suzie and Tommy were in the middle of something they wouldn't forget. No one else needed to look up to make it so. "Get a big cat," she told him as he hailed a cab. "Not a kitten right?" He better not come back with a kitten. Maybe this would be what changed things between them.

When he returned the sky was darkening and the restaurant was almost empty. Sunday dinner shifts were dead, and although her shift was long over, Suzie sat with the two night waiters lighting candles for their tables. Tommy's arms were full, his jacket draped over a cat carrier. "Come have a cigarette with me?" he asked and she followed him down to the basement.

"Check out this motherfucker," he said as he opened the gate on the cat carrier with his thick fingers. "Come on Killer," he said sweetly. "His name was Pickles, but I figured he'd get his ass kicked with a name like that." He made clicking noises, and finally, out slunk a large white Tom cat, his belly low to the ground. He had a torn right ear and one eye was smaller than the other and had pus leaking from it. She wanted to run her hand along the bones in the cat's spine, but didn't want to scare him off.

Killer stayed low, his whiskers quivering and his belly almost touching the floor as he edged along the wall to the shelf of paper goods where he slid beneath and disappeared.

• • • •

They didn't see Killer again for a week.

The waitresses loved the idea of a cat in the restaurant, even if they hadn't actually seen him. They didn't know about the rat so Killer was a source of theoretical delight for them, until after everything went wrong. Even without physical evidence, the waitresses brought in toys and pieces of string for him like they wanted something to take care of. They went down to the basement between shifts and put treats in his bowl to lure him out of hiding. The food disappeared and the waitress with the tits said to Tommy, "See? The cat's fine."

But Tommy gave Suzie a knowing look. "That rat is eating the food," he whispered to her over a cigarette. They smoked outside on the street that whole week instead of in the basement, despite the cold. Suzie hoped that Killer wouldn't solve the rat problem. "Killer better be getting himself ready for battle," said Tommy.

• • • •

A week after Killer arrived at Q, Suzie got a call from Tommy just before five in the morning. She was startled but glad to be the one he called in an emergency.

Tommy's voice was shaky and high-pitched. "It's Killer," he said. "I think the rat got him." He wouldn't say more than that. Suzie didn't push. She fumbled for her glasses and made it to the restaurant as quickly as she could, and by the time she arrived, Tommy had made a pot of coffee and was pacing. The baker was in the back making apricot scones, but she didn't speak English so Tommy didn't bother to whisper.

He ran over to Suzie and grabbed her elbow. "I went down in the basement," he said, "right before I called you. I went down to the basement and I don't know what I saw. I mean, I can't believe what I saw. It can't be what I think it is." He was chewing the nail on his ring finger and kind of laughing. He pushed Suzie toward the basement door with his elbow as he gnawed at his cuticle.

"What did you see?" she asked, but Tommy just held her like a shield against whatever he thought he had seen. She whispered, "Ow," when he grabbed her shoulder, but she didn't shrug his hand away, aware of his need for her at the moment. She was aware in some undefined way that this moment between the rat and Killer (whatever had happened to him), bound her to Tommy in a way that she thought (as only an eighteen-year-old could), would be forever.

As they reached the last step, Tommy pointed at something in the middle of the concrete floor a few feet away. The light, just a single bare bulb hanging from the ceiling, was dim enough that Suzie had to squint, and then had to take a step closer to whatever it was on the floor. Then she said, "Noooo," in a long whisper, like she needed a second, and then without moving she said, "Is that—" She turned to look at Tommy who was biting at the cuticle on his ring finger again.

He said, "It's Killer's leg, isn't it?" He was kind of giggling or even crying maybe. "I mean, it's his leg, right?" He hovered between laughter and hysteria. "Right?"

Suzie turned back, her head tilted to one side like a bird considering a worm, and leaned toward it. Yes. Tommy was right. It was Killer's leg there on the cold concrete, a powder puff of fur with enough weight to pin it to the floor. She felt a surge of fright, as though a rat might come out of hiding and rip *her* leg off.

Tommy said, "I'll go find a clean bucket for the leg," over his shoulder as he took the stairs two at a time.

"Get some ice, too," Suzie said, and her flash of terror subsided.

# Lucky Cat

She told herself to breathe. She was fine, actually. She was fine.

She moved out of her body, then, and understood that Tommy had gone for the bucket because he needed to get out of the basement. It all seemed familiar to Suzie, her down here with the mess, and Tommy upstairs far away from the heartbreak, running around in circles. She could handle this. She *was* handling this.

Tommy came back with a little bucket of ice, which he put down so he could light his Marlboro. The break upstairs had composed him. "Put the leg in here," he said, as though he were in charge. Suzie crawled over and picked the leg up between her thumb and index finger. It was the shape of a small drumstick, fluffy without much blood. She let it dangle there a moment and felt its weight, like a little bag of almonds. She placed the leg in the bucket of ice and reached for Tommy's hand to help her up.

"We need to find Killer," she said, pushing her hair behind her ears and adjusting her glasses. A faint meow came from the elevator shaft a few feet away. Suzie pointed at the gap beneath the door and whispered, "Big enough for a cat to crawl through." Tommy, who's restored courage had already leaked away, was having trouble controlling his hands to get the wad of keys out of his pocket. He shuffled through them looking for the right one. Suzie gently put her hand over his and took the keys, opening the padlock that was meant to keep people away from the grinding elevator machinery.

She pulled the door open as far as it would go to let as much light from the dim bulb into the shaft as possible. There he was. Sinking to her knees, Suzie said softly, "Don't worry, Killer, it's just us." She wanted to call him Pickles instead of Killer, but she didn't want to confuse him. He lay in a little puddle of light, one leg short. "He's alive," she said quietly to Tommy, who was hopping from one foot to the other behind her as she became more deliberate.

The cat's chest moved up and down and he let out a low sound, half hiss and half meow. She could see that his eyes looked glassy and that there was blood here. She took it in, pushing her glasses up again.

77

Tommy started to take off his T-shirt to wrap around the cat, but Suzie said, "No." His T-shirt wouldn't be clean. She said, "Go get one of the clean aprons." Her voice sounded calm to her. In contrast, Tommy's every move was spastic, and she could tell, even in the way that he lunged up the steps, that he was close to tears.

Kneeling by the cat she whispered, "Yes," and, "What a brave cat you are." She leaned closer as she spoke. "What a good cat." She hadn't touched him, didn't want to startle him, knew that when she did touch him, she would have to be ready, in one motion, to hold him so he couldn't get away, that she had to be certain in her actions, and clear. There might not be another chance to save the cat, if there was even a chance to save him now.

Using the same sweet whisper she used with the cat, she said to Tommy when he returned, "Spread out the apron right next to me, nice and slowly, right Killer?" She smiled at the cat even though her face was in shadow. "You're calm, aren't you, Killer? Yes you are."

She took a slow, deep breath and leaned toward the cat, murmuring. The cat, sensing her closing in on him let out a deep, protracted moan. Once Suzie started moving she kept moving, sliding her hands beneath the rice bag of his body, lifting him up just a bit off the floor and swiveling to place him on the clean apron. She kept one hand on top of him, as she used the other to fold the apron around him until he was immobilized and fully swaddled. He did not struggle. "That's right," she murmured as she picked up the white bundle, pushing him against where she thought her heart was. She had heard somewhere that babies were comforted by the sound of a heartbeat.

"Yes," she said, "yes. We'll go upstairs now." Suzie closed her eyes. "You hold on." The cat moaned against her. "Get the bucket," she whispered to Tommy, and they climbed up the stairs and out onto the street. "Hail a cab." She knew to be firm with Tommy now that he was at loose ends. He stepped out onto Hudson Street in the cold morning light and put his arm up in the air, jumping up and down until a taxi pulled over.

# Lucky Cat

"Get in," she said to Tommy gently, and when he sat down, Suzie placed the bundle in Tommy's lap. She said, "Good kitty" which sounded stupid to her, as though she has just said "good kitty" to Tommy, and Suzie realized that her hands had begun to shake. Her chest started to feel full like she might throw up or cry as she watched Tommy cradle the cat's head in his big paw of a hand. Things were shifting again.

Tommy was crying and sniffling as she closed the car door softly. He rolled down the window with his free hand and said, "Jesus Suzie, I love you, you know? Holy shit, right?"

"Right," she said. "Holy shit."

The driver left for the animal hospital uptown, and Suzie stood on the cobblestone street, the sun not risen but the sky pinking-up at the edges. Her trembling was subsiding and she felt the cab pulling away from her, like it was attached to a string tied just below her collarbone, to the cooling spot where the cat had been pressed. She watched the taillights move uptown, away from her, tugging at her like they were trying to tell her something. She went to open the restaurant for the customers who would soon be lining up for their scones and lattes.

• • • •

Tommy called Suzie at home that afternoon. "I dropped three grand on that cat," she could hear him exhaling cigarette smoke into the phone, "and they threw away the paw. The vet looked at me like I was crazy and said, 'Yeah, well, we don't reattach limbs here.' Assholes."

When Tommy brought the cat back to his apartment a few days later, Suzie came to help get the cat settled in to his new, permanent home. "He's back to Pickles," said Tommy as Suzie sat on the floor with the cat in her lap. Pickles looked better in daylight. The rip in his ear wasn't as pronounced as she remembered. The pus was gone from his eye. "Look," Suzie said, rubbing the cat's forehead as he pushed up into her hand, "he trusts us. We didn't ruin him after all."

"It's a fucking miracle," said Tommy, chewing his finger. "Salmon and cream from now on, I swear to God. Salmon and cream."

• • • •

A week after the cat came home from the hospital, Tommy slept with that waitress. He told Suzie he felt he deserved it after everything he'd been through. Suzie said, "Good for you," and she didn't totally blame him. The waitress' breasts *were* spectacular, probably. Suzie saw Tommy differently anyway, or maybe she just felt letdown, or maybe it was something else, a pulling back from the precipice, or an understanding of the water below the cliff, how getting what you wanted was as baffling as not getting it.

Suzie quit the week Tommy slept with the waitress, not because he slept with her, but just because. "I'm not coming back," she told him, "I got a job up by Columbia. It'll just be easier." She felt around in the pocket of her down vest for some gum. "And I quit smoking too," she said, putting the gum in her mouth.

They were standing just outside the restaurant on a sunny Saturday after brunch. There were people all around on the street and a few still in the dining room sipping their breakfast cocktails. Tommy reached over and took the collar of her down vest with both his hands and kissed her right on the lips, nice and slowly, in front of everyone. He kissed her like he meant it, too, pushing the entire length of his body up to hers. "Trident," he said with a wink. "Yum." From her shocked little bliss-cloud, a tiny part of her wished that everyone on the street had seen him kiss her.

Suzie thought for a second that Tommy would try to talk her out of taking the other job, but once he'd kissed her, he seemed complete. She shrugged it off. Suzie knew that Tommy would own the story of the cat one day. At first it pained her that she would be written out, that Tommy would tell it a thousand times to pretty waitresses he wanted to impress. She'd be written out of the story by him, and she came to understand that for the story to work for him, he'd have to edit her out. She conceded, with a momentary and deep sorrow that it would make a better story without her in it.

Still, it was her story too, and she'd tell it later, but her version would have Tommy in it. In both versions, though, Tommy would be the protagonist.

She wound her hair up and clipped it in a bun at the back of her neck before beginning her walk up Hudson Street and decided the next story, whatever it would be, should star someone else, her maybe.

Chinatown—she'd walk up through Chinatown and then head east to her apartment filled with interchangeable girls all looking to begin their lives. Chinatown, yes, she'd walk through China-town, and she would walk slowly and give the hundreds of lucky cats in the windows the chance to wave good fortune at her as she passed.

# Dubonnet

I'm a very private person, which some people might find hard to believe considering I live in the same apartment with my son and his wife and their two children these past three years. But Neil says I shouldn't be on my own, although I don't see why. I can more than dress myself, and by that I mean I have style. And I feed myself. I vacuumed every Saturday and cleaned both toilets every Sunday, like clockwork for thirty-five years.

But you know how it is, your kid says to you, "But Ma, you're seventy-plus, and I got two little kids now, and when you need to go to the doctor or something, I can't just drop everything and come out to Queens to get you, you know?" Blah blah blah. If his father was alive, he'd have a heart attack, me having to leave our apartment after all those years.

My son can be very judgmental, and what I mean by that is that after my husband died, yes, I spent some money on TV things, you know, what you buy through the TV, but I was my husband's beneficiary, which means he left me his pension, and I figured (I still figure) that if I wanted to get a figurine, whose business was it but my own. And so, yes, I got several, but there's no law against it, and I love those things, so beautiful, real porcelain all of them, that pale milky white, like they were made out of snow . . . no, like they were made out of cream. That's it. Cream.

I don't see the point of getting old anyway. You don't get to do what you want like everyone promises, and you have to throw out all your stuff except for what you can fit in your own bedroom. For about half a minute after I moved in, I believed my daughter-in-law when she said that sure, my figurines could be out in the living room, but those kids of hers are a mess, and my son's wife, I don't even like to say her name (which is Cynthia), she doesn't even stop them from running around like maniacs. I'll even say, "You shouldn't let them run around like maniacs," but still my porcelain angel got chipped, right on her wing, and it doesn't take a brain surgeon to figure out how. I got down on the floor and looked for the piece that got chipped off, but no luck. So I brought them all back into my bedroom and put them in my drawer with my pajamas so they would have cushioning.

I asked Neil to put up more shelves in my bedroom, and he said, "Sure," blah blah blah. An entire month went by and no shelves, so I started mentioning it at breakfast, and then I was annoyed because almost another month went by. So I started to up my campaign, I'm no fool, and mentioned it at every breakfast. It's not like I ask for a lot from him. And then I guess things were not going well between Neil and you-know-who, because he snapped at me one morning.

"Can't you ever shut up about the shelves? Can't you ever just ease up?" he said, and too loudly too, so everyone got quiet, except for the little devils, who are going to be in jail by the time they're seven, I swear it, but his wife and Neil and I all got quiet anyway. "Ease up." Where did he learn that? His father would of killed him for saying a thing like that to me.

So I said, "Well I'm sorry to be a bother to you." And I very quietly pushed my chair out, like a lady, and went to my room and wrapped all nine of those figurines in Saran Wrap and then put them in the kitchen garbage can, making sure everyone saw me do it so that no one would put something in on top and break them or anything.

# Dubonnet

The next day was a Tuesday, and when I got back from the park in the afternoon, there was a shelf up in my room and my figurines all lined up very nicely there, all of them unwrapped and in good shape, I might add, except for the angel with the chipped wing who won't ever be whole again, but what can you do? I never mentioned the shelf. I never even thanked Neil because I didn't want to start trouble. So I just pretended the shelves were something that had happened by magic. And I never asked for another thing from Neil, or from her either.

I always liked to go to the park up by my old place in Queens. But now I was stuck in No Man's Land in sort of mid-town only way over east and down a little, in the middle of nowhere with just a dry cleaner on the block and nowhere to get anything normal like a peach or detergent. And my ankles get swollen if I walk too far and so I figured I'd have to make do with the nearest park, which was Bryant. I'd heard it was a mess, but that was years ago, and no, it turns out it was alright, maybe better than alright. I hadn't seen it in a lot of years, and things change, as I know all too well.

So I decided I needed a routine (I've always liked routines as they calm my nerves) and I head there on Tuesdays, to the park and sit and have my lunch by the music. Anyway, the park on Tuesdays is my excuse to get out of the house. Only when I came back one Tuesday afternoon, a few months after I'd moved in, (I know this because the shelves were up by this time), it looked to me like someone had been in my room. I can't say how, but I just knew. I could feel it, like the air had been disturbed in there.

I couldn't sleep that whole night, and I got up twice to check my figurines and they were ok, although I thought maybe that one had been turned, the little girl who was kneeling in prayer, a very holy little figurine with a little cross hanging around her neck that someone must have painted gold with a teeny tiny paint brush, and I swear I had put her on the shelf facing sideways so I could see her praying hands in front of her face in profile, but when I turned on my bedside light and looked up at her from my pillow, I swear she was facing a little bit more toward the wall with her back just a tiny bit to me. I got up and moved her back to profile, but I gave up trying to sleep after that. It made my stomach hurt to think of whoever, the little devils or that woman, or God forbid a total stranger maybe, in my room, the only space I can call my own anymore, when I wasn't even there.

Well, the next morning I went to the phone book and called a locksmith. I have my own money. It's not like I need Neil for money, and I told Neil several times I preferred to live on my own. But you know, blah blah blah, he had a lot of reasons why it would be better for both of us if I moved in, although I'm pretty sure we both regret it now, or at least I regret it, and probably he does too.

Anyway, I got all dressed up and sat at the kitchen table waiting for the locksmith, facing the front door, not even saying a word to the wife. I didn't eat my breakfast—I was too sick from worry. And then a knock came on the front door, and I jumped and so did she. Neil was gone by then, off to his job with the telephone company, and I went right to the door and let the man in and showed him to my room and told him what I wanted. I could hear what's-her-name on the phone to Neil.

"She called a locksmith," I heard her whisper. She was never good at whispering as she lacks subtlety, that one. "Uh huh." I could just picture her looking at her nails. "She better pay for it herself. We're not paying for that." That annoyed me, for obvious reasons. She kept pausing and I peeked out and I could see she was hunched over the phone. "Whatever," she said, and I was right, she was looking at her nails "What does she think she is, Fort Knox?" I thought, screw you. If you ever kept an eye on your filthy kids they'd have a chance in life and I wouldn't have to lock everything up and she wouldn't have to become familiar with the juvenile courts, as I was sure she would eventually. But I didn't say anything.

"Ok," I told the locksmith, "so I'd like two things—a doorknob that locks and then on the inside, one of those hook and eye things that I can latch when I'm in bed at night."

"Yeah," he said, "but you want to be locked in there? It's not exactly safe." He paused as I tried to figure out what he was referring to. "You know, if there's a fire or something, you want people to be able to get in and help you."

I snorted. "I'm not so worried about people trying to help me." That was a laugh. "Don't you worry about my safety," I told him. "These locks are going to make me plenty safe." I started to feel defensive, like if he didn't want the job, there were other locksmiths I could call. But he turned out to be nice and he wasn't judging me, he was just advising, so to speak. He had kind of a gentle look on his face, which was big and round, kind of harmless looking.

"Sure," he said calmly, "sure, whatever you want. I just wanted to mention the fire thing to you." He shrugged. Nice man, really, large in a way that was nice. I sat on my bed all dressed up for company and watched him work. I chatted with him a little, while not being annoying like some people can be. I always liked the mechanical stuff. I was the one who changed the washers in our faucets every year for instance. I was the one. So the locksmith, his name was Primo, it turns out, Primo! So he and I chatted, and it took him a few hours because he needed to do drilling and hammering and all sorts of things, and he gave me a new doorknob that a key could fit in from one side and he even had two different ones for me to pick from so I picked the brass-looking one as it looked sturdier.

I will say that when he first came into my room I was aware, unexpectedly, of how full it was getting in there, and that no one had been in for a while (as far as I could be sure), so I opened up my window nice and wide to let in some fresh air, and I took the figurines off the shelf before Primo hammered and drilled so they wouldn't get rattled. He asked me, "What's your name, anyway?"

I told him, "Dubonnet," which was a lie, but so what? I always liked that name. When I used to get too worried over things, my husband would pour me a drink, and it was usually that Dubonnet with the screw off top, which is now a fancy thing, the screw off top on wine bottles, but back then it was unique. A half a glass of that would do the trick, make whatever I was worrying about move back a little, out of my face. I always thought it was a nice name,

Dubonnet, French-sounding, and it wasn't like I was planning to say it to Primo, but when he asked, that's just what came out.

"Dubonnet," he said, keeping on working, "wow."

"It's French," I told him.

"Primo's Spanish," he said.

"Look at us," I said.

I could see his belly hanging over his pants as he knelt at the doorknob and I thought of my husband, who was always so skinny. Seeing Primo there, so big, I realized that I probably wished my husband had been a larger man. It was very reassuring, is all I'm saying, to have such a large man in the house helping me with my locks when it felt like everyone else was whispering on phones about me and chipping my angels.

Anyway, I turned on my CD player, which I never listened to but I listened to my Chopin sometimes and my Bach, as they calmed me down. Truth is it was my husband who loved the music, so the CDs were his. He had very good taste, my husband. When I'd get nervous, like if he was late coming home from work, and I'd be all riled up and sometimes even crying by the time he got home, wondering what might have happened to him, he'd pour me a glass.

"It's not strong," he'd say, unscrewing the Dubonnet bottle and pouring some into a glass. "It's not like what I drink. This is a drink for a lady," and he'd hand me my glass and he'd pour himself some scotch, and then, if I was particularly in a state by then, before we said a toast or anything, he'd say, "Let's see," and he'd pore over his CDs and he'd say things like, "Bach's Goldberg variations, that's the thing for you," and he'd put it in and hit the play button and then he'd pause, just stand there with his glass in one hand and his eyes closed, and the cello would kick in, and he'd open his eyes and say, "See?" and then, "Cheers." That smile. He always knew how to calm me down, how to help me see right.

Anyway, I saw Primo's belly and I put on the CD and I said, "Bach's Goldberg Variations." Then I added, "On cello," because it said that on the cover. And then I was just quiet. I watched as

Primo finished up everything, and then he asked for a dustpan and cleaned up after himself, like a grown-up. I don't know where I went wrong that I have a grown son who doesn't even put his own dishes in the sink after dinner. My heart would go out to her but she doesn't even say anything, just cleans up after him. Women must be desperate to marry someone like my son and then let him walk all over them like that. Can't even put his own dishes in the sink. What ever happened to women's lib?

That night at dinner, you-know-who asked me for an extra key to my door in case she had to get into my room, but I didn't want to give it to her. What's the point of the locks if she can still get in whenever she wants? "So I can clean in there, at least," she said over dinner, giving a look out of the corner of her to Neil for moral support.

"I clean my own room," I said. Neil took her side, and so I gave her a key from my drawer, I don't even know a key to what, but I didn't care. She wasn't going to get into my room without my permission, and she could fight me or whatever, but I wanted my privacy, and more than that, I didn't want to be up in the middle of the night wondering if anyone had moved my stuff when I was out. I needed my sleep or I'd be a mess for the whole next day, no kidding, crying over nothing, or shaking even sometimes just because I didn't get enough sleep.

So, like I said, the locks made me feel better for a while, but not for forever, and I began to realize that maybe she could have had someone in when I was out on Tuesdays at the park and had a key made. I think you can do that, and she's nothing if not stealthy. So I had to begin worrying all over again with no one to turn to, to help ease my worries like my husband had once been in charge of doing.

So when I went to the park one week, I decided it was best to bring the figurines with me. I took my rolly suitcase out of the closet and wrapped each one of the figurines up in kitchen cellophane, that I bought myself, by the way. I wrapped them up so that if there was even one chip on them, I'd have the piece so that

I could re-glue them together and they could be whole again, unlike the angel who would never have her wing complete, and who I had to turn a certain way on the shelf so that I couldn't see the chip which was too upsetting for me. And I brought them with me to the park in my rolly bag, along with my sandwich, which I ate at one of those little green tables they have there listening to the piano music. That was Tuesdays for me. That still is Tuesdays for me. My husband, it turns out, would have loved that park. I'm just saying.

When I first moved in with Neil, it was winter and the park was only alright. The tree was up and the skating rink, and all of those stores selling handmade soaps I'd never waste my money on. There was a lot to look at, but when spring began to roll around, well that's when it got good, in my estimation. They put out these little catalogues that you could take for free that were full of stuff you could do in the park for no money at all, like French lessons and golf lessons and chess games—you could just ask for a chess set, for instance, from a very nice, skinny young lady who didn't look at me funny, even though I wear a rain hat that I know looks silly on sunny days, but it keeps my hair in place, and some people judge, but the girl who gave out the chess sets did not.

I took the chess set she handed me and sat down at a table rubbing the pieces between my fingers, thinking of my husband who had liked a game of chess. But I had no one to play with, so after a while I boxed the pieces back up and gave them to the skinny girl, who Neil's wife could take a page from. And in summer the lunch-time piano concerts start up, and that's where I like to settle with my sandwich and my bag. And I might even go on a day that isn't a Tuesday, if I feel like it, only that doesn't happen often. But it was there, is the point, if I needed it.

Tuesdays were my day because that's when "she" was out of the apartment for part of the day at school doing something like lunch monitor, although I never asked her what. And so I felt alright leaving some of my stuff there. And I'd make myself a sandwich, and wrap up my figurines and put everything in my rolly bag with some of my hand towels for cushioning, and then, because I invested in some of the larger rolls of kitchen wrap from the Ninety-Nine Cent Store, I'd wrap up the rolly bag too so I didn't have to worry that someone in the park might get into it. I mean, I'm not naïve and what with the tourists in the park, there would be criminals too, and I just wanted to be able to relax.

And so I'd go a little bit early, maybe eleven or so, and find a table in the shade and wipe it off, and then I'd wait until the music started at twelve and eat my sandwich, and it was just heaven, even if the pianist was doing show-tunes or sing-alongs, which were not my favorites, but I tolerated them because it was so relaxing to eat my sandwich there, surrounded by all of those people, listening to music together, with my important stuff with me and nothing to worry about, I reminded myself.

Neil came home one day in the middle of the afternoon, and he and "Cynthia" stood in the kitchen whispering, and it turned out he had lost his job, which I could easily hear because of her volume-control issues. He said he was "downsized," like it wasn't his fault, and maybe it wasn't, but Neil could have a temper, and he never put his dishes in the sink so I could imagine how other people saw him. I tried not to let that show in my eyes since it was a hard thing to lose your job.

When Neil explained it to me, he said that he'd have severance and then unemployment, but I could tell by the way those two were acting so calm, hovering and smiling a lot, that we were in trouble, and that despite the fact that they kept saying, "There's nothing to worry about," that there was in fact plenty to worry about. And I worried about all of it, including that they might ask me for my money, which I wasn't going to give to them. I mean I contributed to the rent and all, but I wasn't going to do more than that, and I had sometimes wondered if they had me move in with them to get my money, and I wouldn't be surprised if that wasn't at least in the back of their minds all along.

So I wrapped up my checkbook and my bank statements with so much plastic wrap that they looked like caterpillars in cocoons.

I went to the bank and made sure with the teller that no one else had access to my account, and then she made me nervous because she said, "You might want to consider giving power of attorney to your son, in case something happens to you." Well, I closed my account about five minutes later. I don't think she even knew what hit her, that teller. I moved my money over to the Chase on the corner and I never told Neil or the other one, either because why would they need to know, not that I trust Chase with all of their trickery in the news, but I'd never be sure if Neil had gotten to that teller and told her to get power of attorney from me. I'd never rest and I knew it the second she suggested it, and that was all I needed to know. I can be very decisive that way. If something's going to keep me up at night, I know to avoid it.

I knew they were strapped, Neil and the kids and her too, and after thinking about it long and hard, one day at breakfast (may I just point out that Neil stopped shaving, which I didn't think would help with interviews, not that I said so, because I didn't) I said, "Would it be a help if I paid a little bit more rent? I could go up twenty-five, if that would be a help."

Well, Neil snorted and said to his wife, "She'll go up twenty-five." I could feel his anger like an earthquake way down deep under the floor. Even though it was a Tuesday when I would normally go out later, I decided to get out early. So I made my sandwich (my hands were shaking the whole time), and I packed up my suitcase with the wrapped statues, which I didn't unwrap anymore so much because why bother. I got dressed in a hurry, and just as I was about to leave, several hours before I normally leave, I decided to bring some other stuff along, seeing how angry Neil seemed. It wouldn't hurt for me to be out of his way, not that any of this was my fault no matter how you sliced it. But anyway.

So I took down a few of my pocketbooks from my closet and in one I put my checkbook , all wrapped up, and then I wrapped some fresh around the purse itself, a nice green purse my husband had bought me on the street, which I've kept spotless, by the way. And in another purse I put my medications, which I'd been doing anyway since I didn't want to worry that anybody had been tampering with my pills. By the end, I had several purses, each with something important inside, like an oyster with a pearl. I piled them on top of my rolly bag, and off I went with my rain hat on to keep my hair nice.

After that, from then on, that was the routine.

Then, maybe a month later, the other shoe fell. I came out to breakfast one morning in October I think, and Neil wasn't there, only her and the two kids, one of whom was throwing Cheerios all over like he was a monkey in the zoo. Who can eat around that? I immediately noticed how bad the wife looked, worse than usual. She looked at me from where she was standing by the sink like she was saying, "Help," and I whispered, "You ok?" She shook her head "no" and started to cry, and those ratty kids didn't even notice their own mother crying by the sink two feet away. She motioned for us to go out in the hall, where she started to whisper too loud as usual.

"He's gone," she practically shouted.

"Who's gone?"

"Your son," she was upset. "Neil, for chrissake."

I was stupefied. I said, "He didn't take the kids with him?" Which was a statement of the obvious, as I noticed a lone Cheerio stuck in Neil's wife's hair, but it was just a thought that came out. She rolled her eyes. She was sort of stylish, I noticed, like, she got all dressed for breakfast, wasn't ever in her pajamas that I saw, not even today, when I might have excused it. For a minute I couldn't remember why she annoyed me so much.

We stood there staring at each other and I started to get nervous thinking about all of things that might happen to us a long time from now. She busted out laughing, which made me more nervous, although I could see her point. I mean, why not laugh? "Where'd he go?" I asked.

"I have no idea," she said. "It's not like he said goodbye or anything."

"Shhh," I said. She was so loud all the time. Then I asked, "Now what?"

"I have to get the kids dressed for school."

"Yeah," I said, "but after that. Then what?" She stood there looking at me with her mouth hanging open. "You can't raise these kids alone," I said, trying to be helpful. "And the rent, for one thing. How're you going to pay the rent?"

"Could you possibly just give me a minute to figure things out?" she said, snapping at me unnecessarily, I thought. I could see I wasn't helping, and I felt very anxious, like I wasn't breathing, like things were going to be asked of me, like I was about to be asked for help that I couldn't possibly provide, and that terrible feeling that comes over a person when she realizes that no one, NO ONE is in charge of things, and just how close to actual doom she and everyone else probably are, just like when my husband would be late from work.

So I went to my room and began packing, even though it wasn't even 8 a.m. yet, but it was a Tuesday, and I just wanted to get out so that I could maybe breathe. My hands were shaking and I tried not to think about Neil, and what an ingrate I had raised. I was looking through one of my bathroom drawers and found an unopened tube of lipstick that I had ordered who knows when on QVC. I had a lot of unopened lipsticks in there, and well, it just seemed as good a time as any to put on new lipstick. So I put it on and it was nice, very pink, like it could give a person an air of confidence. But still my hand was shaking as I tied on my plastic rain kerchief over my hair, and so I did what I hadn't done since my husband had died, which was, I took down the bottle of Dubonnet which was wrapped up on the third shelf of my bookcase. I began to unwrap it, but of course Saran Wrap is hard to unwrap (which is the whole point), and I finally got out my nail scissors and cut it free. It took a second to unscrew the top and then I just took a sip from it right out of the bottle, and took a long deep breath. That was better immediately. I carried it with me into the bathroom to see if my lipstick had been affected by the drink, and it hadn't, so I figured, why not one more sip, and I took one, and just felt like my husband was right there with me. It was nice.

# Dubonnet

I got out the wrap and took one more drink before re-wrapping it, and then when I did wrap it, I wrapped it a bunch of times, so that I'd need the scissors again if I wanted to unwrap it. I was feeling pretty good. My heart was slowing down a little bit, so I put on my Bach CD and sat on the bed to do my socks and shoes, and I left the CD playing as I locked my bedroom door behind me and headed out past her who was getting the kids ready and acting brave. I noticed how, with Neil gone, I didn't dislike her in the same way, like we weren't fighting over anything and the air was kind of leaking out of my annoyance, like we were on the same side of I don't know what all of a sudden.

I got there by ten-ish or maybe earlier and it was nice being in the park so early. The park had a different look to it in the morning. I saw some people I recognized, but mostly it was strangers. My chest felt warm from the drink, and it was easy to not to think about things. As my husband used to say, "Worrying doesn't solve anything," which is so true. I set up my bags on chairs and watched the life in the park sort of wake up, as if it was far away from me, like I was a pigeon or something watching it all from up on a branch.

I watched this derelict guy climb into the fountain and steal the change. Typical. It made me wonder where I had gone wrong with Neil, that he would abandon his family. His father would never have done that. We had hard times, but my husband always came home. But Neil had never been right that way, had never respected the right things, and now here we were with Neil just like this loser in the fountain filling his pockets with wet change that belonged to someone else.

There's a woman I've seen before at lunch time and she's always put together, her hair curled under. Well she was there by the fountain in a chair next to another lady, and I'll tell you what. It was seeing her that practically did me in, because she looked at me, her eyes starting at my head, and I know that my rain hat isn't a big hit style-wise, (although I think of it as like the plastic my aunt used to keep over her couch). Anyway I was used to looks for the hat, so it wasn't that. Her eyes swept down and I thought she'd approve of the lipstick probably, and I'll say this about her, her eyes weren't mean, and they kept going down and then, well she got to my knees with her eyes. I saw her lean over to the woman sitting next to her and whisper something, and then this other woman, looked me over, and despite the Dubonnet my heart was pounding and I just got very still, like I've seen a marmot do on the Nature Channel when it doesn't want a predator to notice it. I just sort of moved my eyes imperceptibly and realized that I had two totally different socks on, both white, yes, but one short and one long, all the way up past my knee. And I was so distraught over this, I don't know why, maybe because I hadn't meant to do it. Like with the hat, I mean to do that, but with the socks it had been an accident, and it sort of reminded me of how Neil and that wife of his and his rotten kids, and his lost job, and the apartment and the angel with the chipped wing, that everything was threatening to fall apart, and I was the only grown up in the room, so to speak, and no one for me to talk to, no one for me to confide in. And like I said, the panicky-er I get, the more frozen I get to avoid detection like a marmot in a tough spot, but my heart was pounding to beat the band all because of my socks. I was so ashamed.

I remembered then that I had a twenty in my jacket pocket and I did something I'd never done before. I packed up all my bags, slowly and carefully so I would appear calm, and it was early, not even twelve yet, but there I was about to fall apart, and look, I didn't know if they'd let me in with all my stuff (some places are not that friendly if you bring a suitcase in with you, I've noticed), but I had to try, so I wheeled everything to the other side of the park, over to the restaurant there and banged my bag up the three front steps. There was this tiny, very chic little girl working the door, like she was eleven years old with short hair like a boy's, and I leaned over and whispered, "Do you think I could just sit at the bar for a quick drink?" This other woman who looked like a giraffe with bracelets up and down her arms came over and made a face like something smelled bad (which I did not), then she and the eleven-year-old leaned their heads together. The giraffe said, "You have money?" She had a British accent, like the Beatles. I showed her my twenty. "And you're not staying too long, right, love? I mean, we're just opening for lunch and it's going to be busy."

She had some nerve, but I didn't want a fight, so I went along. "Right," I said, "Maybe just five minutes, until the piano music starts outside."

"Right then," the giraffe said, looking dubious, and walked away on her very long legs like some kind of wild animal who obviously couldn't wait for me to leave.

So I wheeled my stuff over to the bar, which was pretty much empty, although people were already lining up at the front door to get their name on the eleven-year-old's list for a table. I had to sort of hop up onto my barstool, as I'm not that tall, and the bartender came out and looked uninterested, which didn't help my nerves, and I tried to pull my skirt down a little bit to minimize the difference between the socks. But anyway, I acted confident "May I have a Dubonnet?"

He sighed and said, "I don't know what that is." He did not smile and kept looking around to see if there was anyone else more worth talking to, probably.

I said it again, smiling, "A Dubonnet," but his face stayed blank. How did people stay so unmoved? It was beyond me, like I was a fly or something. Couldn't he see that I was a person? Anyway, I changed tack. "You have red wine, right?" He nodded. I felt I had to hurry as his attention was fleeting. "I'd like a glass of red wine please."

He said, all strung together, "Merlot-Cabernet Sauvignon-Syrah-Malbec-Pinot Noir," again hardly even looking in my direction.

My panic was rising again. "Whatever you think. Whatever is the sweetest." My husband used to tell me that Dubonnet was sweeter than most wine, but what did I know?

"Merlot, then," he said, and then, "trust me." He put an enormous wine glass in front of me with what looked like a tiny little bit of wine in the bottom, but it must have been an optical illusion, because when I finished it and paid (twelve dollars, by the way), I felt just right, light-headed, fuzzy, like I was wrapped up in a down comforter and nothing could touch me. The funny thing was, as I sat there finishing my Merlot I was just staring at all the bottles lined up against the wall, and there in plain sight was a bottle of Dubonnet. I was going to say something, but I was feeling so good, and it was too late anyway. I was just happy to see it there like an old friend.

Anyway, I was a little late to the music, but the pianist hadn't started. There was a table free, not exactly where I like it, but still there was a table, and the wine made it not matter so much that I had to set up my stuff with a lot of people crowded around, which isn't that easy because there weren't enough chairs for me, and finally, I had my bags all set up, and I bent over to roll down the longer sock so that from a distance, at least, it might look normal, you know. And as I was rolling it down, the pianist guy must've sat at the piano because he tapped on the mic and said, "I don't know about you folks, but I'm in the mood for some Bach. Whaddaya say?" A few people clapped, and I just got very still, bent over my sock, like a marmot hiding from a predator. I held my breath and I waited, and then there it was. It was one of the Goldberg Variations. I felt my breath get all caught in the back of my mouth the way it does when I might cry, and I felt terribly lonely, like I had been stabbed with a loneliness icicle or something and it was leaking out into my heart.

I sat up slowly and kept my face very still, but I couldn't stop the tears. I just had a feeling it was a sign from Harry, the music I mean, and I know, I know, that's sort of crazy, to think dead people are giving you signs, and I'm not crazy, and I'm not sure I believe in heaven, which I don't. I mean, I knew it wasn't literally Harry, but I'll just say this, that I knew somewhere in me that it would all probably be ok, whatever happened, and I knew this because of the Merlot (which by the way was delicious) and because of the Bach, like it was all a reminder that the world was pretty much on my side after all, which I tend to forget.

# Dubonnet

I saw that lady and her friend again, the one who had noticed my socks, and she smiled and I could see the kindness in her eyes. She and the other lady with her found a table a couple of tables away from me, and she smiled a second time, and what the hell, I smiled back. Kindness is not repaid very often in this world. I only wished it had been a cello playing, instead of the piano, even though it sounded pretty nice just the way it was on the piano, with cars honking in the background and everything.

I remember thinking that the kids would need me now, that Cynthia would too, and that felt alright, like I could be of use. The piano player hit a sour note, which I could detect because I know that piece of music forwards and backwards, but even the sour note I liked, like it was meant to be. And it's not like anyone else noticed the sour note except for me, and by the time I had noticed it, he had moved on anyway. Isn't that always the way?

# Spring Peepers

Part 1: Nineteen

Like all nineteen-year-olds, she hoped that she was radiant, but knew also that she was deeply flawed (which the entire world might discover any second now). Also like all nineteen-year-olds, she failed to realize that this was the pinnacle of her life, that she would never be more *anything* than she was this very second—never sexier, never more hopeful, never as optimistic, she was as *ripe* at this moment as she would ever ever *ever* be.

It would only be in deep retrospect, decades later, in mourning for what she had once had and misunderstood, that she would understand how natural and complete her perfection had been at nineteen, how all nineteen-year-olds were perfect, really, just buds about to open. By the time she was fifty, she would be able to distill her sense of herself at nineteen and know, with regret, what she had once possessed and unwittingly squandered.

As it was, at nineteen, she behaved with the fraternal twins of profound assurance and crippling insecurity. She was certain, for instance, that that there were no truly catastrophic mistakes, and that she was ready and in a hurry to make a lot of mistakes that she couldn't even name. And again, later, she knew she had been right, that there isn't actually such a thing as mistakes, that every step was a rung in a ladder. So at nineteen, just like that, she dropped out of college and moved to St. Croix, just because, and not knowing that confidence and ignorance were so often the same thing. Nothing would ever be invented or dared without stupidity and bravery.

On the island of St. Croix, she stayed with a friend of a friend and his girlfriend. They introduced her to hard-core veganism, sprouts and soy shakes in the morning, pot and complicated rum drinks at night. He helped her buy her first car, a '69 VW bug sedan hand-painted a turquoise green that the Rastas on the island simply could not get over. "How much you want for that car?" they'd shout at her at stoplights. "I'll give you fifty bucks!"

She learned how to drive a stick shift, and how hard it was to drive a stick shift on the left side of the road, and when a cop pulled her over, she learned that a person's supposed to buy car insurance when they buy a car. "No one told me," she said. He let her go. Thank God this had happened here, where no one would ever see how little she actually understood.

Her first job (outside of babysitting) was at a restaurant in the middle of Christiansted where young waitresses had to wear bright-colored sarongs so they looked like a tourist's lame version of sexy tropical flowers.

At night after the restaurant closed, the wait staff and bartenders stole whatever crappy bottle of liquor the owner wouldn't miss, and drank it on the beach. One night it was peppermint schnapps. They did shots of it and all kissed one another slowly, laughing under the moon, waking in the morning on the beach with splitting headaches, squinting against the murderous sun's stabbing brightness.

Sex was utmost, an adventure, an experiment, a validation and the most daring thing she could imagine. She set her sights on Bobby, an older guy in his 30s who was a frequent customer at the restaurant. He was Irish-looking with red curly hair and freckles, and came in late every night for a scotch. He wore Izods with the

collars standing straight up. It was the eighties. All the other waitresses wanted him and that was why she choose him over the other
guys she could have had.

Her entire strategy was to ignore him. She was pretty sure no
one had ever tried that before, that she had invented the concept of playing hard-to-get. And miraculously, to her anyway, it
worked. When he came in for his drink, she brushed up against
him then turned away and spoke to someone else—simple as that.
By the second night, the bartender said that Bobby had been asking about her schedule, and on the third night, after trying to get
her attention a few times, he walked up to her and just said, "Have
dinner with me."

"When?" she asked.

"You tell me," he said. She said the next night would be good,
but wait, no sorry, that wouldn't work. Maybe next week? His lean
toward her became more pronounced. He was handsome, he really
was, and boy did he like her.

"Call me," she said, and left without giving him her number.
They were both intoxicated by her power.

He came in the next night at the beginning of her shift. She
asked him, "So, what are you doing tonight?" and he whispered,
"Whatever you tell me to do." It made her laugh. She said, "I'm
done by 1:00 a.m." He was parked outside by quarter of.

She followed him in her turquoise VW out to where he was
house-sitting, a palace on a hill with a gray/blue Great Dane who
sat at the outdoor pool with them, one massive paw on top of the
other. The pool was shaped like a lake and was lined with tiny
dark blue tiles. Bobby brought out a bottle of Champagne for her,
a bottle of scotch for himself, and a little bowl of coke for them
both. They swam in their underwear beneath the stars, the Great
Dane looking on, expressionless.

She left a trail as they stumbled through the house to the mas-
ter bedroom. Her purse was by the door somewhere, her sarong on
the floor after that, her underwear (still wet from the pool) slapped
onto the tile floor, her shoes, her earrings all along the way. They

never turned on a light. He began kissing her somewhere just inside the front door, saying nice things, like, "You're too pretty for me." She felt how right he was, how his desire for her conferred great beauty and power onto her.

He tasted of cigarettes and scotch, which was a new taste to her and thus not unpleasant, the way it might have been if she had been a little bit older. His arms were strong and she could feel every single cell in his entire body focused right at her. She loved it. "Look at you," he said, shaking his head and laughing as he kicked off his shoes. "Are you sure about this?"

"Come on," she said, kneeling on the bed, naked, "I'm sure." Before climbing in with her, he took a big drink from the scotch bottle he'd carried in, then crawled to her and tipped her slowly down onto the pillows. She heard the Great Dane sigh and settle on the floor nearby.

Somewhere in the middle of it all, just a few minutes into sex, she became aware of something weird happening, like Bobby was on automatic pilot or something. His body was still moving, but he stopped murmuring to her, stopped holding her face, and almost the exact second that he came, he began snoring, almost before he even finished, while he was still rolling off of her.

She had only been with one other guy, a serious high school boyfriend, and wasn't sure what to do. She said, "Bobby," and poked him, but he didn't respond, leaving her bewildered in the darkness. Then out of nowhere, he made a gurgling noise like he was clearing his throat, turned over, sat up, scratched at the red hair on his chest, smacking his lips together loudly, and said something she couldn't make out.

She heard the Great Dane's nails clicking on the tile floor coming up to her side of the bed. The moonlight made Bobby just-visible as he arose; he walked to the end of the bed and stood there, his feet wide apart. Then she heard it, a steady, strong stream of urine against the foot of the bed. She froze, one hand on the dog. Bobby farted loudly. The stream stopped and then started again. She held her finger up to her mouth telling the dog to keep quiet.

Bobby finished, then got back into bed and began snoring again almost before his head hit the pillow.

She looked deep into the dog's soulful eyes. "Get me the fuck outta here," she thought, and in the dark, she slowly, silently, like a thief, retraced her steps, getting her earrings off the bedside table, feeling around for her underwear, damp from the pool still, and then her sarong and her shoes, and finally her purse.

The dog stood at the front door with her as she tied her sarong back on, looking like "Take me with you." She whispered, "Sorry man," tiptoeing barefoot out into the night, closing the door as quietly as she could behind her.

She was still riled up from the seduction and the cocaine, and reeling from the precipitous devaluation. She was scared too that Bobby might wake up and want to talk or something, God forbid. She rifled through her bag frantically looking for her car keys until she remembered they were still in the ignition. The old VW was facing down the long driveway and she got in, locked the doors, and eased off the hand brake so that it started to roll. Not wanting to wake Bobby, she didn't start the car until she was halfway down the driveway, and then, best as she could in the old car, sped away.

She didn't really know how to get from this part of the island to her place, but St. Croix was small enough, and she'd find her way home eventually. She opened all of her windows, smelling the ocean air and then started up a long, winding hill that the moon was sitting on top of. She took in big whiffs of the night-blooming jasmine, feeling more and more relieved the farther away from Bobby she got, but a growing and massive disappointment was spreading through her chest too.

When she crested the hill, a hill she had never crested before on a part of the island that was virgin territory for her, she was confronted unexpectedly by the neon, belching, terrifying Hess Oil Refinery down in the valley, taking up her entire view. It was lit up like daytime, with several chimneys that threw fire twenty feet into the night sky, a grotesque cross between the Emerald City and some gulag she had read about in high school only last year. She took her foot off the gas and the car stalled, and there she sat at the top of the hill in the moonlight.

There was nowhere to go but forward, so she started the car again and drove, trying not to even look at the refinery as it passed her on the right, mile after mile, stinking of rotten eggs. She didn't know why she was sort of crying, except that everything was just so much lamer than it promised to be. Was it all like this, the being an adult thing?

· · · ·

Bobby came by the restaurant the next day and had brunch with some friends in her station. She gave the table to another waitress, who wanted to know how the date had gone, and of course she didn't tell the truth. She just smiled and shrugged, trying to look mysterious instead of humiliated.

Bobby had his collar up, of course, when he came to her, and put his hands on the bar on either side of her, all smiles. He leaned into her ear and she could feel all the other waitresses watching, which she liked, the being watched, the evidence that she had gotten someone none of the others could have, even as she recoiled inwardly from him, pitied him, hated him a little even. "I'm sorry," he whispered in her ear. "I was kind of an animal last night."

"Yes," she said, "you were."

"I don't suppose you'll ever go out with me again?" he said, still whispering, smiling, leaning.

"No," she said, laughing. "No I will not," aware that to outsiders watching them, she and Bobby looked intimate, and *that* she didn't mind.

"Give me another chance," he said, leaning, leaning. "I could do so much better."

She smiled and blinked slowly. "Not with *me* you can't."

"But *they* don't need to know, right?" He tilted his head toward the rest of the room, at all the pretty waitresses who were watching them. It dawned on her that she had the power to salvage something for them both here, if she handled it right.

"They don't need to know," she said, standing on her toes and kissing him on the mouth, slowly, right in front of everyone. "Now go away," she whispered, and he went, smiling and shaking his head.

She heard him mutter, "Holy shit."

Part 2: Fifty

What a rotten decade her 40s had been. It had taken her father years to die, for one very major thing. At the hospital a few years back she'd seen the worst thing she thought a person could see, her father asleep in his hospital bed, his gown pulled up oddly and his wrinkled pink penis and balls sitting there, stuck onto him like a Mr. Potato Head nose and mustache. "Put out my eyes," she'd joked to her husband. "Put out my eyes."

But it turned out that seeing her father's genitals was not the worst thing she'd see . . . not by a long shot. When he'd panicked, for instance, disoriented and drugged and had crapped on the bathroom wall in the hospital, that was worse, and worse still was that the poor guy knew what he had done and was frantically ashamed.

And worse than that was sitting with him in the nursing home, month after month. When it was time to leave, he'd reach for her hand and say, "How will you know where to find me?" His eyes would get big and watery and she'd sit back down.

"I'll come look for you right here."

"I hope you can find me. I just hope you can find me again." She'd finally have to pull her hand away and go home, hoping all night that she would be able to find him again in the morning. He'd had a place in the heart of New York City, just off Bryant Park, his kitchen shelves overflowing with unopened bottles of Champagne . . . it was hard to reconcile his before and after.

And sadder than all of that even, after he died, was when her mom told her, "I can't hear the spring peepers anymore." Endless, overlapping endings, one after the other, stretching on forever. It made life hard to look at straight-on sometimes, the way everything she loved kept moving away from her.

But it wasn't just her dad's protracted death that wore her out, or her mother's increasing age. Grown-up life was a lot of hard work for almost no reward. The furnace broke or the roof leaked, or just when she thought she was catching up, her property taxes would jump. She was slightly failing at everything, and after her father's death, life had backed up on her like a 10-mile traffic jam. She was fifty and felt like cortisol was dripping from her pores.

At the end of the semester, she would go away, she'd take a year, is what she'd do, to try and let the years of fruitless labor and endless mourning wash over her and away, she hoped. She'd take walks. She'd listen to people. She'd never rush anyone on the road or at the supermarket. She'd try to right herself, however a person did that.

On the final day of the semester, her husband got up early and helped her pack the car. "Don't forget to come back home," he said, nuzzling her neck sleepily in the driveway. His hair smelled like their pillows.

She had a meeting in Virginia the next day and planned to make a trip of it, stopping at a farm in Caseville with a man in his eighties who had been a friend of the family for forever. "With Dad's death," she had written to him, "I feel a constriction of the inner circle, and so I'd like to see you, even if it's just for a cup of coffee." He'd written back, "Come stay at the farm for a night and I'll buy you a nice meal."

She pulled into his driveway in Virginia in time for dinner, the early May sun still hanging in the sky. Peering through the glass front door of his house, she saw him, white-haired and ghost-like. She rang the doorbell but he didn't hear it, so she knocked and shouted, "Hello!" and he turned, smiled, and waved her in.

He had a full head of white hair, preppy clothes and opinions about everything. He was upset, for instance, that his fifty-year-old son wanted to be an actor. "I don't know what to do," he said over his first martini at dinner. "He's throwing his life away."

"He's fifty," she told him, "there's nothing for you to do anymore."

"I like you," he said. "You're terrific," and for a moment she knew he was right. She could see how her laughter fed the old man, echoed the happinesses of his youth. He said, "Oh, I'm having so much fun."

"Me too," she said, and patted his hand, thinking of her dad, gone only a few months.

They split a steak and he said, an impish grin on his face, "How about a second martini?"

"Sure," she said, "what the hell, right?"

Back in the farm's driveway, the moon had risen. He turned off the car and said, "I'm just going to call my girlfriend. Would you say hello to her? I've told her all about you."

"Of course," she said, getting out of the car and stretching. She could smell cut grass and the sky was a lovely navy color with light still behind it like the blue of a stained glass window.

"Oh, Patricia," she heard him shout into his cell phone "we're having the best time. You'd love her. Yes. Yes. Maybe on her way back."

She watched him talk to Patricia in the driveway, and realized that a stream of urine was arcing from his pants, hitting the gravel in a strong, unself-conscious, horse-like jet. She almost laughed, but it wasn't exactly funny, or rather it was the kind of funny that made her wish she was far away. He handed her the phone, and she chatted with Patricia, watching him to see if he had become aware of what had happened, but he gave no indication that he had. He had a wet circle the size of a dinner plate on the front of his Chinos, and when he led her upstairs to show her the room she'd stay in, she saw that he had an enormous wet circle on the back of his Chinos too.

He turned to her on the stairs. "It was a happy marriage," he said down to her, "between your mother and father. Was it?"

"Yes," she said, "yes. They were happy together, right up until the end."

At her bedroom door, she said, "I'll be gone before you get up in the morning so we should say our goodbyes now."

He hugged her, and she hugged him back. She had seen much worse, and would see worse still that she couldn't even yet imagine. Who knew when or if she'd ever see him again, and she'd come to learn that the moments that most make you want to run away were the ones you had to stay for. Proper goodbyes sometimes inoculated you against swarming clouds of regret.

He smiled at her with such sweetness that she put her hand on his face a moment and smiled back, feeling an enormously vulnerable patch of stubble on his cheek that his razor had missed that morning.

She listened while he descended the stairs and could see from her window, which was in a sort of a wing of the house, that he'd turned off his bedroom light almost immediately. She waited another few minutes and then tiptoed downstairs, careful not to make a sound. Once in the car, she locked the doors and eased off the handbrake, letting the car roll halfway down the driveway before turning the key in the ignition. Her heart was pounding. He would be dead soon, just as her father was now. He was already dying, she realized, fleeing in slow motion down the hill. Everyone was already dying.

With many hours to kill before her meeting in Charlottesville, she took the back roads slowly, feeling better and better the farther she got from the old man asleep in the farmhouse. She drove way below the speed limit, her windows down so she could smell the early spring smell of cut grass and turned-over fields. There were deer along the side of the road, bathed in blue moonlight welling up thinly in the night like ghosts.

The best she could figure out to offer was to bear simple witness as the people she loved failed and righted themselves, and failed again. She'd do her best to right herself, now. What else was there for her to do?

She was glad to be driving farther away from home. It meant that, eventually, she'd have to choose to turn around and head back, whenever that might be. Her husband would be there, smelling like sleep. She could hear the spring peepers off in the fields, and a dog barking far away, faintly.

# Dad Died

When I was little, Dad would get into the car and say, "Let's get lost."

"Ok," I'd shout, sitting up in the front seat next to Dad, where kids were allowed back then, no seat belts required.

At each intersection he'd ask, "Which way?" until we didn't know where we were anymore.

"Look," I'd tell Mom when we banged into the breakfast room later. "Dad bought me a diary with a lock and key," or "We threw stones from a bridge into the river."

• • • •

"Dad died," my sister said over the phone. She was crying. "I'm with him. He just died. Dad just died." I could hear other people in the background.

I walked outside to tell our guests at the picnic table in our front yard. "My dad just died," I said and they all reached for me.

I didn't leave right away. What was the hurry? Dad had died. It was over. I sat for a few minutes with my husband and friends. We made a toast to dad. I listened to the wind in the maple leaves, to the guy mowing his lawn across the street, to the blood rustling around in my ears. August. It was August.

Then I left to drive the fifty-three miles across the Tappan Zee Bridge and up the winding road to my childhood home, to Mom and Dad's house where my mother and sister would be.

"Do you want me to go with you?" my husband asked.

"No." I wanted to be alone to cross the Hudson River, to go from when my dad had been alive to the rest of everything else.

I drove carefully, mulling over the sentence, "Dad died."

Dad died. So many d's. Were they plosives? Is that what they were called? I said it out loud. "Dad died." The d's made bursts of air like small, gentle explosions from a cannon filled with feathers. Yes, plosives. Dad died—the d's soft, just T's really, wrapped in spider webs.

Dad. A palindrome—he would have liked that. Dad died. A compact sentence—subject, verb, period. A sentence I had never said before that would be true forever now. Dad died.

• • • •

Dad had been hoping to die since way before the nursing home, and why not? He was unable to stand or walk, unable to feed himself, unable to read. For the final few months, the first thing he'd say upon waking in the morning was, "Oh shit, I'm still alive." No kidding.

He had a dream. "I was trying to sign the check but no one would give me a pen."

"Sign the check?" I asked.

"A check to let me die."

"Oh, how frustrating." I just sat there and held his hand.

"Horrible," he said. "Just horrible."

While Dad was in the nursing home, I worried about him being safe. I pitied him this rotten ending. At night I'd wonder if he was scared or lonely. It's not that I wanted to be there with him, but I didn't want to be anywhere else—there was not a moment's peace for anyone who cared about him at all.

Still, his death was a surprise. When one's father dies, it's always a surprise. I don't care if he's a hundred and fifty years old.

# Dad Died

• • • •

As I inched up to the tollbooth on the Tappan Zee Bridge, I wanted to tell the toll collector what had happened. Shouldn't he know? Shouldn't people be told that everything had changed? I wanted to hand him my five singles and say, "Dad died," look into his eyes for a moment and then drive off, having delivered the sad news.

Instead I was robotic. "Thank you," I said. He took my money without looking up.

• • • •

The youngest of four kids, I was the neurotic one. An insomniac by seven years old, I would fill my bed with books so that if I woke in the night to a silent house I'd have company. One night, as I lay working my way through *Harriet the Spy* (a book Dad had bought me for a nickel at a yard sale), there was a tap on the door. "Are you awake?" Dad whispered.

"Yes," I whispered back. "Come in."

"I couldn't sleep," he said, opening the door, a haggard look on his face. He was an insomniac too, and a reader, and neurotic. "I saw your light on. Want a cheese sandwich?"

We crept downstairs and sat together at the kitchen table in our pajamas, eating cheese sandwiches, two friends who had found one another, against all odds, in the massive, lonely ocean of insomnia.

Later, as the sky was going from black to dark blue, I climbed into my bed, turned the light off, and fell asleep, the crumbling, five-cent copy of Harriet the Spy in my sweaty hand.

• • • •

When he had still been mostly well, before the official diagnosis, before the nursing home, we liked to carry our lunch into Bryant Park and sit under the plane trees with strangers. We'd listen to the live piano music. He was a New Yorker, Dad was, but he couldn't walk far anymore, couldn't remember simple things, like how elevator buttons worked, so we would make the increasingly

115

bewildering trek downstairs to the lobby and across 40th Street right into the park, like it was ours, like it was filled with our guests. He'd smile at the music. He'd reach for my arm and say, "Isn't this magic?"

People die slowly, I understood much later. They don't die in an instant like they do in the movies. It happens in the most infinitesimal steps—in tiny, barely perceptible stages. He was beginning to die even then, listening to the music in the park, although I only realized it later.

• • • •

He stopped making much sense in the final months in the nursing home, the line between reality and hallucinations blurring. "There's a man in a field," he said to me one day. We were sitting on the smoker's patio overlooking the Hudson River. It was a sunny afternoon, and I thought the sun might warm up Dad's always-cold hands. "He's standing with his legs apart, his hands on his hips. He's shouting."

"Is he friendly?" I asked.

"Oh yes."

"What's he shouting?"

"He's shouting for me to come to him." Dad closed his eyes and I thought he might be falling asleep. Then, in a wobbly voice, his eyes closed, he sang stanza after stanza after stanza of a song I'd never heard. When I was a kid, we used to sing in the car together when we were trying to get lost. I thought I knew all of the songs that he knew, but of course, how could I?

If I interrupted, he might lose his train of thought and stop singing, so I kept still.

The sun beat down on our clasped-together hands. The river below pushed past. The Hudson seemed very old, and I thought how it had been there before either of us, and how it would be there after Dad was gone, and after I was gone too.

"I can't remember the rest," he said and we opened our eyes. "What's wrong?" he asked. He mimicked my expression because it lay in front of him. He knit his eyebrows together like mine. His eyes teared up.

"Nothing's wrong, Dad. It's just nice to hear you sing."

He began to pick imaginary threads from his shirt and hand them to me. I took a few and then told him, "You can drop the rest on the floor. The nurses will sweep them up."

"That wouldn't be right," he said, "to throw them on the floor for someone else to clean."

• • • •

After the Tappan Zee Bridge, I took back roads the rest of the way, roads Dad and I had biked once. I felt like my heart was wrapped in a thousand, paper-thin blankets, beating somewhere outside of my body.

I knew that the moment one's father died was something a kid owned, and I was still his kid, regardless of my age. It was mine, his death, and I was aware from somewhere outside of myself that this was a rite of passage, something whose effect I would only later understand, and only maybe, even then. It was mine alone yet also something that connected me to every other person on earth. I mean, everyone's dad died, right? Eventually?

As I got closer to home, I passed neighbors' houses, but those neighbors hadn't lived in those houses for decades: Mrs. Whitfield's house, the Rowells, the Giovincos, the Sloans. Everyone I knew was gone. People I'd never met lived there now. I turned on the radio and then turned it off. Everything but my heartbeat distracted me.

• • • •

He hadn't always been perfect. I had hated him for saying mean things to my sister when she was trying to learn her multiplication tables. He was bossy and moody and unpredictable, and rotten to boyfriends, really rotten. Later on, though, he asked me over and over again to forgive him. By then I had my own life, and he had mellowed and I wasn't mad at him anymore. We were friends by the time he began to apologize.

117

A few weeks before he died, I told him, "I think about you here and hope you're ok. I think of you all the time." He sat there a minute. I couldn't tell if he had understood me.

Then he leaned forward the tiny bit that he was able and paused. "It's time," he said, "to stop thinking about me."

I was irritated at first. "I don't want to stop thinking about you," I told him.

"I should have been dead a long time ago. It's time you stopped thinking about me now." He nodded and, leaning back in his wheel chair, closed his eyes. He was right. I needed to make my own mark. He was headed away from me, in a different direction from where I was going.

• • • •

I drove in second gear past the nature center where we used to sing Christmas carols with neighbors. That memory hurt, like it was a kite tied to one of my ribs, tugging at me, pulling me backwards toward a suffocating nostalgia.

I drove along Spring Valley, a road so narrow that the August vines seemed to reach for my car, trying to yank me backwards.

Then I turned up the road to Mom and Dad's house, which was now just Mom's house, I realized. As I neared it, the feeling of being pulled back and back by the vines and the kite in the strong wind of the August afternoon intensified.

Dad died, I realized anew, and my desire to be a child again welled up with such sudden force that I felt the kite string strain and strain and strain, and then SNAP! the freed kite lofting up and up into the windy blue sky. The vines seemed to retract as I pulled into the driveway. I turned off the car and sat there feeling his absence like it weighed something. It was time to stop thinking about him, but I'd stop thinking about him later.

I remembered, as I sat there with the motor off, how getting lost with him had been such fun. "Right, left or straight?" he'd ask at every intersection. As we'd get farther away from familiar terrain, he'd say, "We're totally lost now! Boy, I hope we can find

118

our way home!" and we'd laugh at that, because it was exciting to be lost together, and because we'd always found our way home eventually before.

# Patience and Fortitude

It was around six-thirty, so the train was full of freshly showered, Type-A commuters, the ones who are at the office before everyone else, the killers. And it was insane in Grand Central, like ants running over each other. Veronica tried not to look happy, tried to soften how crazy-excited she was to get her summer in New York City started, but still, she shimmered.

She took the 6-train uptown to the Andres', had been on the subway before, just never without her mother, so she drank up the weirdnesses there that morning: the way that all the men were taking up two seats with their spread-apart legs, the women in their pretty shoes, and the crazies screaming through with their hands stabbing out for money. She felt connected by her very-own-edge-of-hysteria, everyone rocking in this giant, screeching cradle, no one making eye contact, manic charm radiating off of everyone. Total Heaven.

Veronica was hurrying because the Andres (sort-of-friends of her parents she'd met only once when she was home from boarding school) would be leaving for work by seven. She wouldn't officially start nannying until the next day, but they wanted to get her set up today, and she wanted to make a good impression by being early, if possible. She got off the subway, turned the wrong way, and then had to retrace two cross-town blocks. Finally she texted Mike, "found it!!!" regretting all the exclamation points the second she'd sent it, all her enthusiasm for everything making her feel so fucking young.

The doorman, a pudgy quiet guy, carried her bag to the elevator and said, "The Andres are up on twelve," which she knew, but she was so electrified that his small shred of kindness weighed about twice what it normally would. She said, "Thank you," and tried to transmit with her eyes how on-the-verge-of-incredible her life was. He smiled in at her as the doors closed.

She examined herself in the elevator mirror, noting her cute sundress and very cute short haircut, completely overlooking the intense vulnerability that pulsed out through her eyes. And that smile. Like a lamb to the slaughter.

When she got to the apartment everyone was running around. Mrs. Andre worked at the U. N. and was "very important," according to Veronica's Dad, who had used air quotes. That's why the Andres were leaving at the end of the summer, for Mrs. Andre's job. Mr. Andre was a lawyer. His hair was alarmingly slicked back, liked he's just come up from being underwater.

Mrs. Andre, who was pretty Type-A, was texting as she handed Veronica a binder full of lists: emergency numbers, foods that Maddie could eat, foods Maddie <u>MUST</u> avoid, maps of Manhattan and Central Park, train and bus schedules. "We keep classical music on at all times," she said. "It stimulates Maddie's brain development." Veronica had done enough babysitting to know that the Andres were going to Baby-Einstein this kid to death, and Veronica knew that the kid would hate her parents eventually, or disappoint them, or both, probably. There was no living up to Mozart. A two-year-old would have to blurt out the quadratic equation to justify Mozart being played to them in their crib. Anyway.

Veronica looked up from the binder to see Mr. Andre roll his eyes at her like he knew how over-the-top his wife was, even though he was clearly in on the whole exceptional-child-thing. Parents who were forever pushing, and then trumpeting their kids' smallest achievements, were the worst, as Veronica knew. They were the last ones to actually care if their kids were happy. Getting decent parents was so entirely the luck of the draw. She'd been lucky. They were ok with her being a nanny for the summer. The Andres would never let that happen to Maddie.

As Mrs. Andre (who seemed terribly thin swimming inside her blue suit) was going out the door, Mr. Andre yelled after her, "So do we want to introduce her to the child then?" like his wife was an idiot, although who knew what she was coping with at the U.N.—Ebola, world peace? Mrs. Andre smiled like a diplomat and led Veronica into Maddie's room.

She was only two, Maddie was, with brown curls and chubby cheeks. Prima, this grown woman, was getting Maddie dressed, and winked at Veronica. Even though Prima had to wear a uniform, she'd managed to have her personality bust through with these really long nails painted like American flags. Veronica watched the toddler being dressed by the older woman and took in the warmth that some women transmitted to one another—not Mrs. Andre so much, who hadn't yet really looked at her.

Veronica wanted to hang out with Maddie and Prima, but Mrs. Andre took her elbow and said, "Your room's over here. Be back for dinner—Six o'clock?" She smiled at her phone and was gone.

"Which was my room?" Veronica asked Mr. Andre. He pointed with his thumb, then stood at the kitchen counter sipping from one of those tiny espresso cups and looking at his phone, totally sealed-off in his own little atmosphere.

Veronica dragged her bag to her room and when she came out, Mr. Andre was gone and Prima was giving Maddie a toaster waffle. Prima said, "Veronica, right? Listen, *m'ija*, you got the day off. Don't waste it here," so Veronica threaded the apartment key onto the necklace Mike had given her, and left Prima there chatting at Maddie in Spanish.

It wasn't even seven-thirty when Veronica asked the doorman, "Which way is Fifth Avenue?" He pointed, smiling. They were kind of friends already.

123

• • • •

As she headed downtown, she took in the pricey menus, the guy walking seven dogs, the expensive, hushed-looking hair salons. She'd never been alone on Fifth Avenue before.

The people were well-groomed up there, but not attractive exactly. They looked like, if they ever laughed, they'd be laughing *at* someone, like they lacked essential warmth. Veronica, on the other hand, was purposely kind, as a way of bribing the universe to be kind to her in return. She was young enough to still believe in reciprocal kindness.

She checked to see if Michael had texted back, but no. They'd been talking less and less since graduation. He'd moved to California for college, but he had talked Veronica into the concept of them-as-a-long-distance-couple so persuasively that her hopes were really up. And he was popular, athletic, had made her parents love him—he was *that* guy. It had occurred to her, though, that she had leaned more toward him than he had towards her. She could just feel it and was forever trying to pretend to lean away. The thought embarrassed her enough that she said, "Whatever," out loud, and then, "Anyway."

"Nanny?" he'd asked. "You're going to be a *nanny*?"

"It's just for the summer," she said, but she'd gotten the message.

"Well, don't fall in love with anyone in New York," he'd said from California. She should have known something was up, with how much it had never occurred to her to fall in love with someone else until he'd said that.

She texted him again. "moved in! Wish u were wme!" As soon as she sent it she regretted it, could hear the clanging of her exclamation points. His opposite-of-neediness had a way of making Veronica's exuberance look pale and lame, like the wrong haircut.

Down Fifth she went, along Central Park. Everything seemed to be coming to life in front of her, warming up and opening. She watched the pretzel guy outside the Met crank open his red and white umbrella, and tourists gathering on the steps in the sun next to the pigeons and the splashing fountains.

She walked past the museum, and down past the Plaza Hotel where she'd had a kid-drink with her dad a million years before, as a celebration of something she'd forgotten. It had been served in this ceramic Tiki-cup-thing with a paper umbrella stuck in it. She still had that glass.

A couple of years after this, after the nannying was over and Veronica was about to graduate from college, Veronica would watch a drunken woman in a fur coat throw her cigarette into the carpet of The Plaza, then put it out by crushing it with her expensive pointy shoe into the carpet, and then stumble away. As soon as Veronica saw that, it would get bound to the memory of the Tiki-Cup, and to the memory of this hopeful morning walk she was taking down Fifth, and it would subtly change those hopeful memories to sad ones—sad because the hopefulness of the naïveté of the Tiki-Cup and the hopefulness of the walk would be ruined by the cynicism of the lit cigarette thrown into the hotel's carpet by a rich, careless drunk. So later, the drink, the cigarette smoldering in the carpet, Maddie and what happened to her, and Mike and what happened to them, were all braided together in a tangle of care and careless that she would never unsnarl. The lipstick-stained cigarette smoldering in the Plaza's carpet became a symbol she'd never interpret correctly.

But that day as she walked down Fifth, she was thinking about how her father had gotten her that drink in a Tiki-cup to probably try to inoculate her against the later stuff that life throws at a person, that he had been doing that parent-thing of piling up the good for his kid as a hedge against the inevitable crappiness of the world, against the way people could think so amazingly little of a person, could be cruel to even people they loved—especially to people they loved.

Still, that day, although she had some nagging doubts, Veronica felt the Plaza, and the city were hers, and that everyone she

125

passed could tell how much she belonged. Down she went, past Atlas with the world on his shoulders, and then down past Saint Patrick's Cathedral, which, even with scaffolding in front, gave her goose-bumps. Her mom, who'd grown up in the city, used to think that they were saying "Lead us not into Penn Station" when they said the Lord's Prayer. Veronica's dad had said, "When you see Penn Station, Ronnie, you'll understand." She was pretty sure she was nowhere near Penn Station at the moment. Tourists were swarming this part of Fifth, all looking up.

Most of the Type-A's were already at work by the time she reached the New York Public Library with the lions out front: Patience and Fortitude. Those were their names according to Veronica's mother. It was like her mom to know their names. Her mother paid attention to little beautiful things, like the names of the stone lions, little things that, which, when piled together, added up into what actually mattered.

Then came the Empire State Building. Already, by nine, people were lined up to go in, excited and hopeful, like they were about to see something in person that only existed in their dreams. They were all leaning towards each other. Sweet.

She checked her phone again. Nothing. She knew by the way Mike tensed up when she reached for his hand in public that he didn't like it, like he wished Veronica could be more like him. It made her wish she was more like him too, and less like how she was, which wasn't the best feeling, to always be trying to tamp down her own enthusiasm to make Mike like her more.

Around Fourteenth Street, people started to have rattier clothes and more piercings. There was a coffee shop with a cardboard sign in the windows that said "vegan lattes" written in crayon. Veronica saw an older woman (thirty maybe) wearing the exact same dress Veronica was wearing, which made Veronica feel great. The woman was on a bicycle and you could just tell she didn't care what anyone thought of her. She had tattoos up and down her left arm.

Fifth Avenue ended at Washington Square, where two girls

sat on a bench. One had tons of eyeliner and black Army boots, the other had shaved blue hair and torn-up fishnet stockings. Veronica loved them for how unapologetically pissed-off they seemed. A guy roller-bladed past playing an accordion, and another guy was playing "Imagine" on his guitar. It was *that* kind of park, full of pot smoke and accordions and Army boots. It felt so honest, felt so much more "Veronica" to her than the Upper East Side had.

She looked at her phone again and still nothing, so she sat down on a bench and called Mike. A girl answered, which confused Veronica into silence. The voice said, "Do you know what time it is?"

It was a little bit past nine, maybe nine-thirty but Veronica didn't answer because she was thinking. It dawned on her that it was earlier in California (which she'd forgotten . . . *again*). Like. A lot earlier. "Is Mike there?" Veronica asked.

The voice didn't answer, just said, sort of annoyed and sleepy, "Are you the one who's been texting all morning? Who *is* this?"

"Who's *this*?" Veronica said, with more confidence than she felt.

The Voice just sighed, like *Veronica* was bothering *her*.

"Why are you answering Mike's phone?" Veronica started to sweat everywhere, even in the crook of her elbows.

"I live here," she said, "with Mike."

"With Mike?" Veronica asked. "With Mike Carpenter?" Maybe The Voice was mistaken. "Like as his roommate?"

"Jesus. Like as his girlfriend. Is this Veronica?" How did she know Veronica's name? The Voice yawned and said, "I assume this is Veronica? Maybe you should stop calling."

Veronica watched the guy with the accordion fly past again. She did not like him anymore. "Is Mike there?" she said.

"Seriously," the Voice said, "you should stop calling him probably." She waited and Veronica waited, and then they both clicked off.

Veronica hit re-dial, sweating now in earnest. She got his

voice mail (thank God) and said, in a stupid, fake-light-hearted voice, "I just had the weirdest conversation with someone who says she's living with you." Pause, pause, pause. "Call me, ok?" Pathetic. Her heart was racing.

She put on her sunglasses to give herself distance. She was sweating through her T-shirt and leggings and right through her sun-dress. Fifth Avenue seemed shitty now, like it was where she had been stupid and happy, so she walked over to Sixth, going from anger to shame to denial in jagged little circles as she walked. She told herself, "I'll never speak to him again," even though she was holding the phone in her sweaty hand, in case he called.

As she walked up Sixth she told herself that she could probably sleep with Mr. Andre if she wanted to, the way he had been rolling his eyes at her, and he was just the kind of guy who'd sleep with his nanny. The thought of other guys wanting to sleep with her made her feel, momentarily, less disposable.

The buildings on Sixth Avenue seemed taller, like they were keeping the sun from her. After a while she looked up from her feet and there was a park filled with pots of overflowing pink flowers, like a mirage.

People were playing golf (crazy!) in this tiny park, and people were sitting in big brown chairs like they were at their cabins in the Adirondacks and not in the middle of New York City. She walked into the park and past the people in chairs, past all the people lying on blankets on a green lawn, and up a few steps and, what the hell? There was a sea of people doing yoga. So odd.

She watched, leaning against the pedestal of a statue of Gertrude Stein, and remembered the line "A rose is a rose is a rose," which she'd read in AP English. It had seemed pointless then, but with what had just happened, Veronica felt like she finally understood what the poem, and everything else on Earth, meant. Totally. A rose *is* a fucking rose, she thought.

The people doing yoga were on identical pink mats, with the yoga instructor teaching them how to do a Sun Salute. Then someone was handing her a rolled up mat. She thought she had to pay, but the guy (who had braids in his beard) said, "It's free," so she unfurled her pink mat.

"Now for Downward Facing Dog," said the instructor-lady, who wore a little microphone headset so everyone could hear her. "Breeeeeathe." She stretched out the word. "Let's get down on our mats on our hands and knees." Veronica's dress was in the way, so she lifted it off so she was in her leggings and T-shirt. She took off the necklace with the key on it, too, realizing how much she had always hated that necklace, with its cliché interlocking hearts. It was so totally impersonal. God, Mike was an idiot.

"Your hands," the instructor continued, "should be ahead of your shoulders." Veronica looked up to make sure she was doing it correctly. "Goooood. Now curl your toes under, and when you exhale, lift your knees from the ground." Up her butt went with everyone else's. "With your next breath, push your heels down to your mats and feel the stretch along the backs of your legs." Veronica pushed her heels down, trying to be careful, knowing that focus was the thing with yoga. "Breathe into your belly button," the instructor said, and Veronica breathed into her belly button with complete concentration, as though it might change something.

Why hadn't she ended it first with Mike? This is what she was thinking about. That sleepy woman on the phone was closer to Mike already than Veronica had ever been—had answered Mike's cell phone—probably didn't care whether Mike held her hand in public or not. Life must be so much easier, Veronica thought, when you didn't care. When had they moved in together? Jesus. They were living together? It was hard to believe. "Breeeeeathe," the instructor was saying.

When they lay down on their mats and looked up at the sky, Veronica had a thought that seemed to telescope through to her future self, as though she could almost predict that lit cigarette in the Plaza carpet too. She hoped, as she lay there, that this thing with Mike wouldn't somehow ruin her, while knowing that it already had. It was one of those injuries, though, that you couldn't see. She wouldn't know for a long time how it had fucked her up. God, the whole thing pissed her off and hot tears fell down to her ears and onto the pink mat. It pissed her off so entirely.

She did her best to stay in her body and breathe, but she kept seeing herself as an old lady, still haunted, like Miss Havisham who died a spinster in her rotting wedding dress in *Whatever-That-Book-Was* that they'd read in AP English. As they crumbled up into Child's Pose, Veronica was relieved to hide her face in her knees.

Everything felt ruined.

Afterwards she went back to Fifth and into St. Patrick's. She wasn't religious, but church sounded comforting. Inside, the light was blue from the sun coming through the stained glass windows. She watched someone pray, then got on her knees, put her hands together and bowed her head. Not knowing what to say, she asked, "Why?" which seemed like a sort-of-a-prayer, but the question just hung in the cool room like a dust mote, unanswered.

She knelt there, aware that she hadn't been perfect either, not as bad as Mike, not like moving-in-with-someone-new-while-still-calling-yourself-someone-else's-boyfriend, but somewhere on the spectrum of unkind. Cruel world, she thought. Sad, cruel, stupid world.

Then she lit a candle for herself, which she was pretty sure was not how it worked. Those candles were for people who had died, but it was all she could think to do. She slid a quarter in the box to pay for the candle where it made an echo-y little metallic *plunk* as it fell to the bottom with the other coins in the locked brass box.

She took the subway back up to the Andre's only this time the guys taking up two seats seemed like real assholes. There was a baby crying, and suddenly his mom just lurched him up in the air out in the aisle facing away from her, and he threw up on the floor while everyone watched. The people nearby tucked their feet under their seats. What else could they do? The mother got off at the next stop without even trying to clean up anything. People really sucked.

As Veronica walked from the subway, she kept checking her phone, but nothing. She passed a guy asleep in a doorway with a big gray beard and a winter coat. She imagined all of the sweat that had probably collected in that coat, and what the water would look like if she washed it for him, how dark the water would be with everything he had been through, how she'd have to rinse it and rinse it before the water came clear—if the water ever came clear. She slipped a dollar under his elbow.

She checked her phone again, as if Mike calling me might re-animate her. But he didn't call. Could thinking that Mike had loved her when he had been in love with someone else make her un-reanimatable? That's what no one seemed to understand— that people could be broken beyond repair, that not everything bounced back like they did in cartoons.

When she got home, the doorman smiled and put his hand up to his hat. At the mirror in the elevator she lifted up her sunglasses and looked at herself to see if it was obvious that something delicate had been crushed to death in her, but no, she looked the same, only she had more freckles now from all the sun.

When she got in the apartment, something Mozart-y was playing. Prima said, "Hey there," and Veronica noticed Prima's faint mustache. "I'm putting her down for her nap," Prima said, "and then let's have some coffee." She was probably the same age as Veronica's mother.

Veronica sat at the kitchen table, lay her head on her hands and wished she wasn't the kind of person who lay her head down on a kitchen table when people were cruel. Pathetic.

She thought how her sorrow would seem like failure to her parents, who had done what they could to set her up for happiness with their Tiki-Cups and knowing the names of the library lions. Veronica didn't want them to know how totally she'd screwed up the happiness thing they'd wanted her to inherit. She thought about the careless people in *Gatsby* (high school again). There weren't enough Tiki-Cups in the entire world to inoculate a person against the human tsunami of carelessness. She would forever be knocked down by that stuff. Jesus.

She finally stood up and looked into Maddie's room. Maddie was smiling up at Prima, and Veronica, thought, *Maybe she hasn't been ruined by her parents yet.*

When Prima came out to pour the coffee, Veronica handed her the necklace. "You want it?"

"You don't want it?" Prima asked.

"No," Veronica said. "It's from my ex."

"Oh," said Prima. "That explains your face."

Veronica laughed. "Your nails are incredible," she said.

"Sick, right?" Prima put two mugs of coffee down, and stirred like six spoonfuls of sugar into hers. "Wait," she whispered, "you want some?" She took a joint out of her uniform pocket and wiggled her eyebrows.

Prima lit up and passed it to Veronica. "So when did it end?" Prima asked.

"Like an hour ago."

"Ha!" She saw Veronica staring at her phone. "Seriously, *m'ija*, you should turn that thing off for a while."

"I know, but what if he calls?"

"Right," Prima said, "but even if he does call, he can't unbreak your heart, right?" They sat there for a while, staring. "Listen," said Prima, putting one hand (warm from her coffee cup) over Veronica's, "some broken things never get fixed. I'm serious as a heart attack."

"Right," Veronica said. "Right."

Prima got up to refill her coffee cup.

The apartment felt warm and quiet with just the three of them there, Maddie asleep, Prima fussing with the coffee. Veronica felt like she'd never been as young as Maddie was, and knew she'd never be as old as Prima. She felt their heartbeats around her, smelled the coffee and the pot in the air, but knew in her deepest heart that what she was going through was unique.

Prima sat back down holding the coffee pot. "A heart that hasn't been broken isn't worth shit, anyway. Trust me. Turn off the phone."

"Right," Veronica said, not completely understanding. "I'll turn it off," she said, slipping it into the pocket of her sundress. It was on vibrate, so she'd feel it when he called.

# Next Time

By 6:30 in the morning, the streets of midtown Manhattan were roiling. May, who hadn't been in the city for months, stood on the stoop, stunned, while her mother slept upstairs. In a few hours they'd be settling her father's estate, surrounded by lawyers, and May, as usual, hadn't been able to sleep.

She hesitated, trying to figure out how to enter the river of men and women rushing past in their suits and sneakers, their earbuds in, staring down at their phones, taking up the entire sidewalk, purposefully oblivious to the world around them. The doorman stood next to her, drinking his coffee. "They are in such a rush," he said to her, smiling, lifting his paper cup to indicate all of humanity.

She didn't want to leave the doorman's side. It was upsetting lately, the depth of the unkindness around her. May felt terribly vulnerable ever since her father had died, as though good and bad had tilted precariously when he had gotten off the see-saw and gone wherever people go.

May thought about going to the new bakery over by Fifth. She'd seen their pistachio éclairs in the window many times but had never gone in. Next time, she kept telling herself. Next time. But they looked expensive covered in a pale green glaze the color of matcha tea and caked with toasted pistachios. They wouldn't be open yet, and anyway, an éclair at 6:30 in the morning? It seemed indefensible. Being in New York City made her want things she hadn't even known existed, and made her want them with force.

It was still so early that there was time before her mother got up. You would think that Le Pain Quotidien would be open. But no. May had forgotten all of the schedules in the months since they'd been to the apartment, so she read the sign in their window. They wouldn't open until seven, which didn't feel soon enough. The wait staff stared out the window like drowned cows, looking at all the customers-they-wouldn't-have who would go somewhere else.

Fine, May thought, she'd go to the corner of Sixth, to that fluorescent PAX with all of its cut up fruit in plastic boxes. It was the grapes that brought home the sadness of store-bought fruit salad, their navels brown and beginning to rot the minute they were plucked from their umbilicus. And the lighting at PAX was harsh, too bright and cheerful, like tourists trying to blend in while standing in the middle of the sidewalk always looking up, in everyone's way.

When she got there, she remembered the way the cashier at PAX was way up high like she was on a throne of fruit salad. May had to reach way up to pay for her coffee, which she couldn't pour herself but had to ask the throne lady to pour for her. "One coffee light with half and half."

"Size?" the woman asked. Clearly, she hated May. Size? Oh God. There was a line forming behind her.

"Medium?" May asked. The woman on the throne sighed deeply without looking at May. "Small or large?"

"Small," said May smiling, wishing this woman would like her. She couldn't really win anymore. People hated her before they even knew her, before she even walked in the door.

And then came the receipt. Receipts. Jesus Christ. Now you got a receipt for a cup of coffee, for a pack of gum, shoved at you, hundreds of them a day, aggressive helpfulness.

# Next Time

What were customers supposed to do? They were supposed to order loudly and immediately, and then pay right away, and then take the change, the receipt and the cup of boiling hot coffee and get the hell out of the way so that the next person in line, who already hated them for taking so long, could scream his order at the woman on the fruit salad throne while she looked at her cuticles or the ceiling, or rolled her eyes at a co-worker. How could old people survive like this? May thought of her father being handed receipts, and him moving so slowly those last years, when he was still able to walk at all. How could anyone rush an old, sick man like that? She hated to think of him, vulnerable as those naked baby hamsters she'd seen at the pet store, alone in this city. She almost couldn't bear it.

The receipts made her feel constantly, frantically inundated with tiny things that didn't matter, a distraction from the fact that the world was falling apart. If May left the receipt on the counter, it was an act of aggression, wasn't it? She was not the kind of person to litter, and leaving it on the counter felt like littering, like saying to the woman on the throne, "You clean up the mess." Then again, taking the paper felt like succumbing, like she'd agreed to something she'd never meant to agree to.

Today, she left the receipt on the counter, exhausted already, her heart pounding, defeated and it wasn't even 7 a.m. when she crossed back to the park. She could see the park employees in their green uniforms waiting for the last minutes to tick by before removing the chains that barred her entrance.

May held her warm cup in both hands and breathed. She saw a man asleep on one of the park's steps. He was well dressed in khaki shorts and a pink, seersucker, short-sleeved shirt, a lot like the one her mother had purchased the day before at Orvis, on sale for forty-nine dollars. But his feet were bare, and May could see from the caked dirt and thick callouses there that his life was not in any way about pink seersucker shirts, as he lay curled in the fetal position on this chilly-ish October morning. She looked to see that he was breathing. He was. The morning had already been too much

137

for her, and she felt like if she could be a kid again, if she could just have a do-over, a lot of suffering could be avoided if she were only more thoughtful this time around. Her heart was pounding. *Thump thump thump*. She wanted to see the man's face, but worried that he might be someone she knew.

Finally one of the green-shirts unhooked the chain separating May from the park. She took her first step up toward the enormous planters, overflowing with pink and green begonias, and her shoulders fell an inch. She'd watched the pigeons eat every flower off a box of begonias the last time she'd been in the park. Who knew that pigeons ate begonia flowers? Her shoulders fell another inch as she stepped up into the park's atmosphere. Oh, thank God the park was open. She wiped at her eyes with her free hand. Thank God for this park, for all parks.

May plunked down where she and her mother liked to drink their morning coffee, in a plastic Adirondack chair near the fountain, the South West Porch, it was called. There was a blond couple standing in front of the fountain taking pictures of themselves. *Tourists*, she thought, pulling back the plastic lid of her coffee. Their sneakers and camera looked expensive and they were very tall. *German tourists*. They were the worst, all "me first," all elbows and no humor, striding around the city like gods.

In her twenties, May had lived in TriBeCa way before it had its film festival, and she'd lived in Park Slope before it was filled with twin strollers. She knew how un-cool mid-town was, had even sneered at it herself once, but still. Her father's slow death had exerted a gravitational pull toward Bryant Park where he could easily go. She did not choose midtown. It's what she had been handed. Fitting, she thought, for a middle-aged, overweight woman.

As she sat in her chair, she thought of her mother upstairs asleep. Since her father's death, May had gone into pre-mourning for her mother. She had begun to worry about all sorts of new things. When it snowed, for instance, May felt anxious until her husband made it back from work to their home in New Jersey. She hadn't been a worrier before her father's death, but her inner circle had become so enormously constricted when he died that she felt herself clinging to things. She could no longer, for instance, bring herself to delete any of her mother's emails.

In her secret heart she fantasized about what a relief it would be when they were all dead, everyone she loved. There would be nothing left to lose when her husband and mother died, nothing that life could hold over her head any more, nothing more to worry about. She could drink at dawn if she wanted to, and dye her hair purple, neither of which she would ever do, but still, she could. It could snow ten feet and she wouldn't care. She'd just sit and watch the cardinals and chickadees hop from branch to branch.

She looked around the park, sipped at her coffee and watched a man sitting with his little boy at a table near the fountain. The father was feeding strawberries to his little boy, who slouched down in his chair, chewing without looking up.

May's mother had her own gravitational pull. Even in her eighties, people fell in love with her. At dinner the night before, they had gone to a French bistro, and the *maître d'*, an older French guy with a large moustache, took May's mother in his arms and danced her to her seat. How would May ever survive without her? She had been beautiful, her mother had, but now that they were both so much older, May understood her mother's charm was from her lack of cynicism, her steady capacity for wonder.

"Oh," her mother (a lifetime New Yorker) had gasped, on their walk back to the apartment after dinner, "How beautiful the Empire State Building is, just in its plain white light like that. Isn't it wonderful?" May wanted to feel that sense of delight, but she knew that what she loved about her mother, she herself could never possess.

May sat in the park and watched her mother's "leaf guy" come toward her. He pushed a garbage can on wheels and swept up the piles of October leaves, one at a time, into his dustbin, which he tipped into the garbage can from time to time. *Jesus*, thought May, *He never stops.*

She wondered, with all of his sweeping up, what his house

looked like. He seemed pretty tidy, but maybe when he got home at night he was sick to death of sweeping all day. Maybe he had Chinese food containers all over the floor, and gum wrappers. Her mother would argue that he kept his apartment neat, that he was a good, hardworking husband. That's what her mother would say. May thought he could just as easily have bodies in the basement. Who knew?

A man wearing torn black pants walked past. May could smell him, could see his toes poking through the front of his filthy sneakers. He looked to the left and right and then climbed right into the fountain, where he bent down and began pulling change up from the water where tourists had thrown it making their febrile tourist wishes. What on earth did tourists wish for? Good room service? He squatted in the water, pulling his dripping fists up like pistons, and shoving the coins into the pockets of his wet black pants. The man with the strawberries saw him and bustled his family to a table farther away.

May looked around. There were usually security guards in the park. Shouldn't someone stop this guy? On the other hand, maybe he needed the money, although there was something grotesque about him squatting there. A policeman stood off to her left. Good. Let it be his problem. But he was facing away from the fountain, texting.

He was probably hungry, the guy in the fountain.

May watched Mr. Leaf Sweeper come around. Maybe he'd say something to the thief. But he didn't. He kept his eyes down, sweeping up the big, thick plane tree leaves that kept falling. She twisted around but the cop hadn't looked up from his phone yet. Oh well. Maybe the guy in the fountain could get a moment's peace from the money. Maybe he could get a pistachio éclair or a pack of cigarettes or a place to sleep. Maybe there was enough money in there to change things for him. Could money do that? Was there enough money in all of the fountains in the world to change things? However large her father's estate was wouldn't matter, not really, not in a life changing way, would it?

# Next Time

When he stood up, his pockets were noticeably bulging. He sat on the edge of the fountain, swung his wet feet out and walked away, leaving big wet footprints on the flagstones as he went past the cop and down the steps, and was absorbed back into the writhing sea of people heading for work. May was glad to be in the park and not out there.

Her heartbeat settled almost back to normal. She ought to bring a cup of coffee up to her mother, but the park was so pretty, full of flowers still in October. She hated to leave. Once she left the park, it was on to lawyer's office on Park and the finalization of her father's will. It would all be over by noon. No more death certificates would be needed. Obituaries and condolences were already a thing of the past, and with this, his life, in the eyes of the law and the bank, would be officially over, in triplicate. There would be nothing left to arrange, nothing left to manage or fuss over.

From where she sat she could see the statue of William Cullen Bryant sitting up on his marble statue, his back pressed against the New York Public Library. No one knew who he was anymore. No one even looked up at him. That's what happened when people, even famous people with parks named after them, died. They disappeared.

She breathed and sipped and thought about that pale green éclair in the bakery window. She'd get it for herself, later, after the lawyers', no matter how much it cost. She might never have the chance again to buy a pistachio éclair, and she didn't know what she was waiting for. They probably had a special little box they'd put it in. They would be friendly in the bakery, she imagined, taking pride in what they'd made, caring about a customer who would spend whatever they charged for a kind of éclair they had probably invented. She would definitely get one of those today, and May would say to the woman behind the counter (in the friendliest way) that she didn't need a receipt.

She'd do it after they were done with the lawyers. She would bring her mother there and let her choose whatever she wanted, and May would buy a pistachio éclair, and they'd carry their pastry into the park and listen to the live piano music and eat their little treasures near the pots of begonias. By then, in just a few hours, her father would be dead for real, and then, maybe, May could eat a pistachio éclair and think about what, if anything, might come next.

# The Absence of Sound

Timothy stood at the fountain, his hand inside his coat pocket rubbing two quarters against one another. He'd walked past this fountain on his way to work at the library hundreds and hundreds of times, and had never thrown his money in, but today he did think about it. Although what would he wish for? There wasn't anything to wish for exactly.

He had gotten up in the middle of the night, as usual, getting a bleary-eyed drink of water in the dark and visiting the bathroom, and realized only in the morning that he had not heard the sound of his cat Bipsy's paws trotting behind him. She was old, but still she followed him everywhere. How had he not noticed the absence of that particular sound? It was as though he had failed to notice the stopping of his own heartbeat.

He'd felt all strangled inside when he figured things out. *Now what*, he'd kept thinking as he made the coffee and packed his lunch for work in silence. *Now what?*

Timothy looked up at the branches of the London plane trees overhead in the park, and could see birds everywhere, busy busy busy. April was the right time for them to be swooping between treetops and lampposts, hopping on the ground for muffin crumbs. He mourned never learning their names. His mother and brother had known the names of birds, but he'd never latched on. They could tell one song from another, could look up at the under-wing of a bird lofting up like a kite against the blue sky and say, "peregrine falcon" or "turkey buzzard" in hushed and intimate tones to one another. He was never part of their circle, but had watched from the side, a tiny little circle of his own, intersecting nothing.

Timothy could tell a seagull (white) from a crow (black) from a cardinal (red). He'd studied an illustration of a stork in a Hans Christian Anderson story, but his knowledge wasn't advanced enough for him to be certain whether or not there was a difference, say, between a crow and a raven, or between a stork and an ibis, a heron or an egret. Heron and egret and ibis and stork might all be different names for the same thing, as far as he knew.

It was too late now to wish for the intimacy of family. His mother was decades gone, and his brother had gone off to Kuwait a long time past, and had come home essentially gone years before he'd died. Something had shaken his brain loose, is how Timothy had pictured it, and everything that had been his big brother had effervesced like the escaped air from inside a popped bubble.

The loss of Timothy's cat made the loss of his brother fresh again, made the absence of the whispers between his brother and mother echo, reverberate as though Timothy was standing in an enormous, empty room. They had been easy friends with one another, his mother and his brother, but Timothy hadn't decoded the language of their intimacy. Their closeness had been like a promise of eventual closeness for Timothy that he could not bring to flower.

The birds around him now were babbling. April was cruel, he thought, just as Chaucer and Eliot had promised back in college. The flower pots in the park were full of hyacinth and daffodil bulbs, their buds bursting up through the dirt like aneurysms. The bunched buds swelled up and unfolded their redolent petals until they sagged open, calling to bees. He could almost hear the birds above puffing out their chests, their songs like screams, hopping onto one another's backs to fight or mate. The park was positively indecent with procreation.

# The Absence of Sound

He sank, contented in his own invisibility, and watched.

Just do it, he told himself, and took both quarters out. *Plash* and then *plash*. He didn't wish for anything, just thought *Bipsy* and then *Bipsy* as each coin sank beneath the water and rested on the cool stone bottom.

Timothy hid his face down inside his coat's collar as he walked around the fountain and onto the gravel path. He knew that beneath his feet were the two floors of library stacks, what had been called the Bryant Park Stack Extension, that the employees of the library called BIPSE. It's how he'd come to name his cat. It was spectacular down there, well-lit and every inch waterproofed, a self-sufficient world of temperature and humidity controls, filing cabinets, microfiche and moveable shelves. And twenty-six feet below *that* (he had been told) there was a stream, carving its way through the cold dark rocks that held the city up.

If you turned it all upside down, there was as much unseen beneath New York City as what lay on top of it. And as much inside each person Timothy passed as all of it combined.

He sank inside his own indistinctness and walked past the new sod, rolled out each April after the skating rink was heaved up, packed on trucks and put into storage for another year. At the 40th Street loading dock entrance to the library he held up his ID card. Manny said, "Morning" and Timothy raised his hand in a wave, curling up the corners of his mouth to approximate a smile.

His little desk seemed far away as he slipped down the side stairs where he wouldn't likely see anyone, through a door where he had to swipe his ID card, down the long white hallway (more like a brightly lit tunnel) and past the vault where special books were held. He wasn't allowed in the vault, with its John James Audubon original double-elephant folio from the 1800s, and William Blake's engravings from *Songs of Innocence and Experience* from the 1700s, touched by the artist's very own hands. Blake had written "A robin red-breast in a cage/puts all Heaven in a rage." Timothy knew what robin red-breasts looked like. They were self-explanatory. There were documents in that vault that were so important that Timothy wasn't even allowed to mention them. And the people allowed in the vault had to wear white cotton gloves if they meant to touch anything.

Down and down he went, where the smell of reinforced spines of old books on thick paper reaching him like violets. He could breathe here. And think. The only noise the hum of the purring temperature and humidity controls. As the space grew narrower, Timothy felt better. Down he went to the second floor (the lower of the two), edging his way between the wall lined with microfiche cabinets and the stacks to where he had arranged his desk to be maximally hidden. Finally he was alone.

He had a coat rack that the guys in the carpentry shop had given him where he hung his coat, umbrella and briefcase. When he'd first gotten the job, almost forty years earlier, his mother had made him one of those little stamped labels with his name on it, and so Timothy's full name was glued near the handle of the briefcase. Every time he saw it he felt a soup of nostalgia and pity for his mother, so long gone, and for himself too. He knew it was sad for a man in his sixties to carry a briefcase with a label from his long-gone mother that was peeling up at the edges. But what was he supposed to do? Pry the label off and throw it out? For what? For whom?

He sat down, turned on the computer, and straightened out the NYPL pins he had arranged at the base of his desk lamp representing his ten, twenty and thirty years of service. He was due another pin soon. Then he downloaded the book requests he'd received. It was only 9 a.m. and there was an enormous list of books to pull and send upstairs. It would be a blessedly busy day.

• • • •

Later, as he was eating his cheese sandwich and checking for new requests, he heard a shout approaching from far away. "Timmy!" It was Lloyd Calaban, he of the glossy black hair and easy laughter. Everything seemed so easy for Lloyd, who was able to glide through life without worrying, it seemed. It was hard to imagine

Lloyd, for instance, waking up at three in the morning, suffocating from loneliness. Timothy was aware that his own pallid face and high-arching eyebrows could discomfit people. He tried to soften his face, to make himself look less surprised by squinting his eyes before Lloyd came around the corner. The squinting sometimes helped, but the way his hair had thinned and receded made him look like a sinister clown. Timothy stood up to meet Lloyd, and then thought better of it and sat back down. Too eager.

"I know you're here somewhere," Lloyd called.

"Yes," Timothy croaked, standing up and then sitting down again, clearing his throat. "I'm here!" He tried to sound as though he'd been speaking to people all morning. Lloyd started around the corner, all smiles, and Timothy met him with a sudden wanting-to-be-known by him. He wanted to tell Lloyd, for instance, that he had a collection of seventy-three antique book marks at home, and that he knew how to play the recorder, and that he had eaten caramels at his aunt's farm in upstate New York one summer as a boy, but he said nothing.

He felt especially isolated around Lloyd's expansiveness, which trumpeted out ahead of him like a red carpet that Lloyd himself rolled out wherever his feet went. Timothy wanted Lloyd, or someone, to know how much he loved his job, and that he'd had a cat named Bipsy for seventeen entire years, and that he was encouraging to her about how pretty she was, and how safe he'd keep her. He wished Lloyd could have seen them together watching *Jeopardy!* every weeknight, Bipsy on the back of the couch, reaching out one paw and resting it on Timothy's shoulder.

Lloyd came toward him like a sun-shower. "Tim-MAY! How's it going, man?"

"Oh, just fine. Busy morning." He couldn't think of anything else to say, felt a blush coming up his face.

"Listen," said Lloyd, "could you help me out? I'm being pulled in a million directions and Melanie needs this, in her hand, ASAP."

Timothy reached his hand out for the request slip. "I'd be happy to," he said.

"She's mad at me," said Lloyd, grinning, leaning against the metal microfiche cabinet. "Fixed me up with her sister and, well, you know, those things never work out, but I want to give her time to cool off, and she wants this like yesterday, you know?"

"Yes, yes, I can do it for you."

"But, like, you have to do it now, buddy. I'm sorry to ask you to do this. I'm sure you're in the middle of other stuff."

"It's no problem at all," said Timothy, heat rising up through his cheeks and past his pale, high eyebrows.

"I owe you one, buddy," said Lloyd, pointing his finger like a gun at Timothy and winking, "I owe you one."

"No, no," said Timothy, beaming. He loved the idea of Lloyd owing him one. When Lloyd had gone, Timothy tried out the gun hands, and then went to find the book that Melanie needed. She was efficient, Melanie was—neither friendly nor unfriendly, but busy and no-nonsense. She was important, had to deal with board members and donors. If she needed this book right away, he'd get it for her. He felt like Superman.

"I'm on my way," he said under his breath, giddy, rushing to the stacks. There he pushed the button that separated the shelves from one another. He could hear the mechanism *whir* as the shelves slid apart, creating an aisle for him. Timothy's focus was laser sharp as he ran his finger along the numbers on the shelves until he came to the right place, pulled the cardboard sleeve out and found Melanie's book. He put the request slip inside the front cover, hugged the book to his chest, and rushed out of the stacks and up toward the public part of the library, his pulse racing.

Timothy walked quickly through the tunnel, up one set of stairs and the next, and then over to the main part of the library, just below the first floor. He slowed as he reached the busy lobby toward the Fifth Avenue entrance near the famous lions, Patience and Fortitude, and stopped near the top and peered up into the crowd of people; the guards at the revolving door checking bags, the sunlight pushing weakly in, the homeless man who came in every lunchtime and slept in the reading room for an hour, and dozens and dozens of people looking up and zig-zagging unpredictably in and out toward the main exhibit, or up the stairs or toward the gift shop, just like the birds in the park.

He blinked and tried to soften his face, knowing that he would look spectral to anyone who turned and saw his pale, startled head floating there. He imagined how scary that might look, and forced himself to keep moving up. And as he thrust himself forward up the final stairs, his shoe-tip caught the lip of the top step.

And he flew.

For just a moment.

Up through the air.

In slow motion.

Melanie's book flew, too, up above him, the pages fluttering, and he thought how the book looked like the bone in "2001: A Space Odyssey" tumbling end over end. Timothy reached his hands out as though he were an athlete of some kind, a quarterback maybe, and caught the book as he slid under it along the stone floor and came to a halt, his eyes shut, his heart pounding, time returning to normal speed. He could hear people gathering around him cooing, and wished he could melt away under the eyes that he felt feel staring down at him.

"You alright?" It was a woman's voice nearby. He opened his eyes. A pale fiftyish woman leaned over him, her eyebrows knit in worry, her lips a bright matte-orange slash in the middle of her face. Her hands were fluttering like moths around him. She knelt down next to him and for the second time that day, he felt a blush rising up in him as he lay there clasping Melanie's book. "You ok?" she said, patting his hand.

She'd touched him. He became very very still. "You ok?" She was smiling and he felt a surge of love well up in him for the pumpkin orange of her lipstick and the way she had no real chin, and for her hands, trembling like bird's wings do when they are in a bird bath.

He blinked once, twice. "My cat died last night," he told her. There, he'd said it, and could feel the ribs in his rib-cage loosen.

She leaned closer and her lips made an O. "She was curled up in a ball this morning, her tail over her nose." And then, as though she had asked him a question, he said, "Bipsy. I called her Bipsy."

The woman smiled.

"She was seventeen years old. I got her after 9-11 from the pound." His mouth felt very dry and he stopped talking and blinked up at her. He should probably try to get up. He wondered if he should tell her that, not knowing what else to do, he had finally put the cat in a plastic Food Emporium bag and thrown her down the garbage chute, but he decided to keep that to himself.

"Hey," she said, still smiling down at him, but starting to unkneel. "Hey! I know you!" Her eyebrows came together as she tried to figure out where she knew him from. "Yes, yes, I *know* you." His heart quickened and he felt tears in his eyes. She *knew* him? She knew *him*? "You threw money in the fountain this morning. I saw you." She had seen him, and she saw him now. She could see him.

She laughed and held out her hand to help him up, and the crowd that had gathered backed up a step.

"I saw you is all," she said. "What are the chances of that, that I'd run into you twice in one day in this city?" She turned to no one in particular and said, "What are the chances of that? I see this guy throwing money in the fountain this morning, and the next thing I know, he falls right at my feet in the library?"

The group was dispersing, but a few responded by shaking their heads or murmuring to one another before turning away. He felt all their circles intersect, or felt the pull of their now-separating circles.

The woman with the orange lips said, "Maybe I'll see you around." She smiled a real smile that made her eyes crinkle up, and she touched his shoulder. "Crazy city, right?" He nodded and blinked against the wetness in his eyes.

Timothy slipped behind one of the massive columns to peek back around at where he had just been lying, at the way the sun poured in over the moving people, how every second was like a snapshot, a new one each moment.

He should have told her about how he could play the recorder, and about the caramels he'd eaten at his aunt's that summer in Upstate New York. But memory was a kind of accomplishment in itself. And if he'd run into her twice in one day, perhaps they'd be thrown together again. He rested his cheek against the cool marble pillar. He remembered, then, why he was upstairs, and he hurried to deliver Melanie's book to her.

•　•　•　•

As he passed the fountain on his way home that evening, he stopped again. Way back on 9-11 he had almost thrown money in. That had been the only other time he'd even considered it. *The subway stops at Bryant Park.* That's what people always said, but on 9-11, when they let everyone out early from the library, he had crossed through the park on the way to his Hell's Kitchen walk-up. It was at the fountain that he'd become aware of the lack of sound and vibration under his feet. The subways weren't running for the first time in his whole life, and there was a stillness he couldn't fathom, like a penny dropped down a well that never splashed.

There had been no way in or out of the city that day, and he had stood in the silent park with a handful of pennies ready to throw into the fountain as a gesture against hopelessness, but he'd been waved away by the National Guard with their guns, everything deranged and toppled together in his mind. The fires and the fallen towers smelled like burning rubber, and like concrete smashed into bits light enough to float, and like the scent of unsettled souls. Were there particles of people in the air? Of course there must have been.

Hi awareness of the silence of the stopped subways beneath the park had never dissipated, and now it got layered beneath the missing sound of Bipsy's paws thumping down off the couch behind him. The space of her absence would make a palpable presence of its own, like the repercussive silence of the subways, and the music of his mother and brother whispering the names of birds back and forth, call and response, while he stood apart and listened.

# Acknowledgements

The Virginia Center for Creative Arts (VCCA), the MacDowell Colony, and Cill Rialaig all gave me time and space to write. They believed in my work before I did, and put me in close proximity to fine artists who became friends and inspirations. What they provide to artists strikes me as some of the most important work there is.

Dan Biederman of the Bryant Park Corporation, and Angela Montefinise of The New York Public Library helped me research the magical and hidden world beneath Bryant Park. Craig LaCaruba and Gennaro Oliva gave of their time and expertise as well.

I am grateful to Rosemary James and Joseph de Salvo of Faulkner House Books for recognizing my work early on, and to Patrick Perry, the editor of *The Saturday Evening Post*. He is a fine and generous editor, who I hope to work with again.

Leapfrog Press chose to publish this, my first book, and in so doing helped make my dreams a reality. The enthusiasm and intelligence of Lisa Graziano and Rebecca J. Schwab made the process a delight, showing me how very collaborative writing can be.

Old friends Dorry and David Swope gave me time to write out on Wauwinet, a magical place. Known for their quiet generosity, Dorry and David make me feel optimistic.

Phillip Cioffari, a writing professor of mine, taught me a great deal. Many of the stories in this collection were conceived for his classes, and were improved because of his feedback. He told me, "Successful writers don't give up"—advice that I lean upon often.

Three friends in particular (fine writers all) read the stories in this collection and gave me their insights: David Ebenbach, Daniel da Silva and Martha Witt. Not only have they made me a better writer, they have made the process of revision pleasant. I owe them forever.

# The Subway Stops at BRYANT PARK

My permanent cheering squad is made up of my mom Anne Moss, my sister Liana, my high school pal Shay Craig, and my friend and neighbor Barbara M. Walker—lifetime stalwarts all. I can't help thinking that my father, Lloyd Moss, and Grandma Hastings (both gone now), are part of this squad, regardless of their lack of physical proximity.

As for my husband Craig, well, he doesn't like compliments, and I wouldn't know where to begin anyway. Suffice to say, then, that everything good and happy in my life begins and ends with him.

# Publishing Credits

"Omeer's Mangoes"
    Winner of *The Saturday Evening Post's* 2015 Great American
    Fiction Contest
    Winner of the Faulkner-Wisdom Gold Medal for Best Short
    Story, 2014
    Anthologized in *The Best Stories from The Saturday Evening
    Post* 2015
    Named in the Glimmer Train Top-25, Fiction Open 2014

"Sky View Haven"
    Originally appeared as "Eagle View Haven" in *The Blue Lake
    Review*, 2013
    Republished in *The Blotter*, 2015

"Beautiful Mom"
    Published in *The Westchester Review*, 2013

"Lucky Cat"
    Short-Listed: Faulkner-Wisdom Competition for Best Short
    Story, 2014
    Published in *Cahoodaloodaling*, 2014
    Nominated for a Pushcart Prize

"Dubonnet"
    Published in *The Stockholm Review*, 2015

"Spring Peepers"
    Nominated for a Pushcart Prize, 2015
    Published by *Prime Number Magazine*, 2015

"Dad Died"
>Originally appeared in the anthology *Grief: A Life in 5 Stages*, 2014
>Republished in *Ars Medica* out of Canada, 2016
>Republished in *Hospital Drive*, 2015
>Winner of *Lunch Ticket's* Diana Woods Memorial Award in Creative Nonfiction, 2015

"Next Time"
>Published in *Crossroads*, 2016

"Milagro"
>Published in *SAND Journal* out of Berlin, 2016

"The Absence of Sound"
>Published by *Neworld Review*, 2016

# The Author

Photo by Mahmoud Sami

N. West Moss has had her work published in *The New York Times*, *McSweeney's*, *The Saturday Evening Post*, *Salon*, and elsewhere. Her work has received two Faulkner-Wisdom gold medals (for fiction and nonfiction), The Diana Woods Memorial Award for Creative Nonfiction from *Lunch Ticket*, and *The Saturday Evening Post*'s Great American Fiction Contest. Her stories have been nominated for two Pushcart Prizes. She is a fellow at VCCA and MacDowell, and she's at work on a novel, set in New York City, and a collection of poems.

For upcoming readings and publications,
visit her Website at:            nwestmoss.wordpress.com
or follow her on Twitter at:     @scoutandhuck
or on Facebook at:               N West Moss

## About the Type

This book was set in Adobe Caslon Pro, a typeface originally released by William Caslon in 1722. His types became popular throughout Europe and the American colonies, and printer Benjamin Franklin used hardly any other typeface. The first printings of the American Declaration of Independence and the Constitution were set in Caslon.

Designed by John Taylor-Convery
Composed at JTC Imagineering, Santa Maria, CA